SECRET OF THE
SUMMER SCHOOL
ZOMBIES

Librarian Reviewer
Katharine Kan
Graphic novel reviewer and Library Consultant, Panama City, FL
MLS in Library and Information Studies, University of Hawaii at
Manoa, HI

Reading Consultant
Elizabeth Stedem
Educator/Consultant, Colorado Springs, CO
MA in Elementary Education, University of Denver, CO

STONE ARCH BOOKS
www.stonearchbooks.com

Graphic Sparks are published by Stone Arch Books
151 Good Counsel Drive, P.O. Box 669
Mankato, Minnesota 56002
www.stonearchbooks.com

Library of Congress Cataloging-in-Publication Data
Nickel, Scott.
    Secret of the Summer School Zombies / by Scott Nickel; illustrated by Matt Luxich.
    p. cm. — (Graphic Sparks. School Zombies)
    ISBN 978-1-4342-0760-9 (library binding)
    ISBN 978-1-4342-0856-9 (pbk.)
    1. Graphic novels. [1. Graphic novels. 2. Schools—Fiction. 3. Zombies—Fiction.]
I. Luxich, Matt, ill. II. Title.
PZ7.7.N53Se 2009
[Fic]—dc22   2008006710

Summary: Trevor thought nothing could be worse than spending the entire summer in
school. Then his teachers turn into homework-crazed creatures! Now Trevor and his friend
Filbert must find a way to stop the zombies. Or they'll be trapped inside the classroom of
doom forever!

Art Director: Heather Kindseth
Graphic Designer: Brann Garvey

1 2 3 4 5 6 13 12 11 10 09 08

Printed in the United States of America

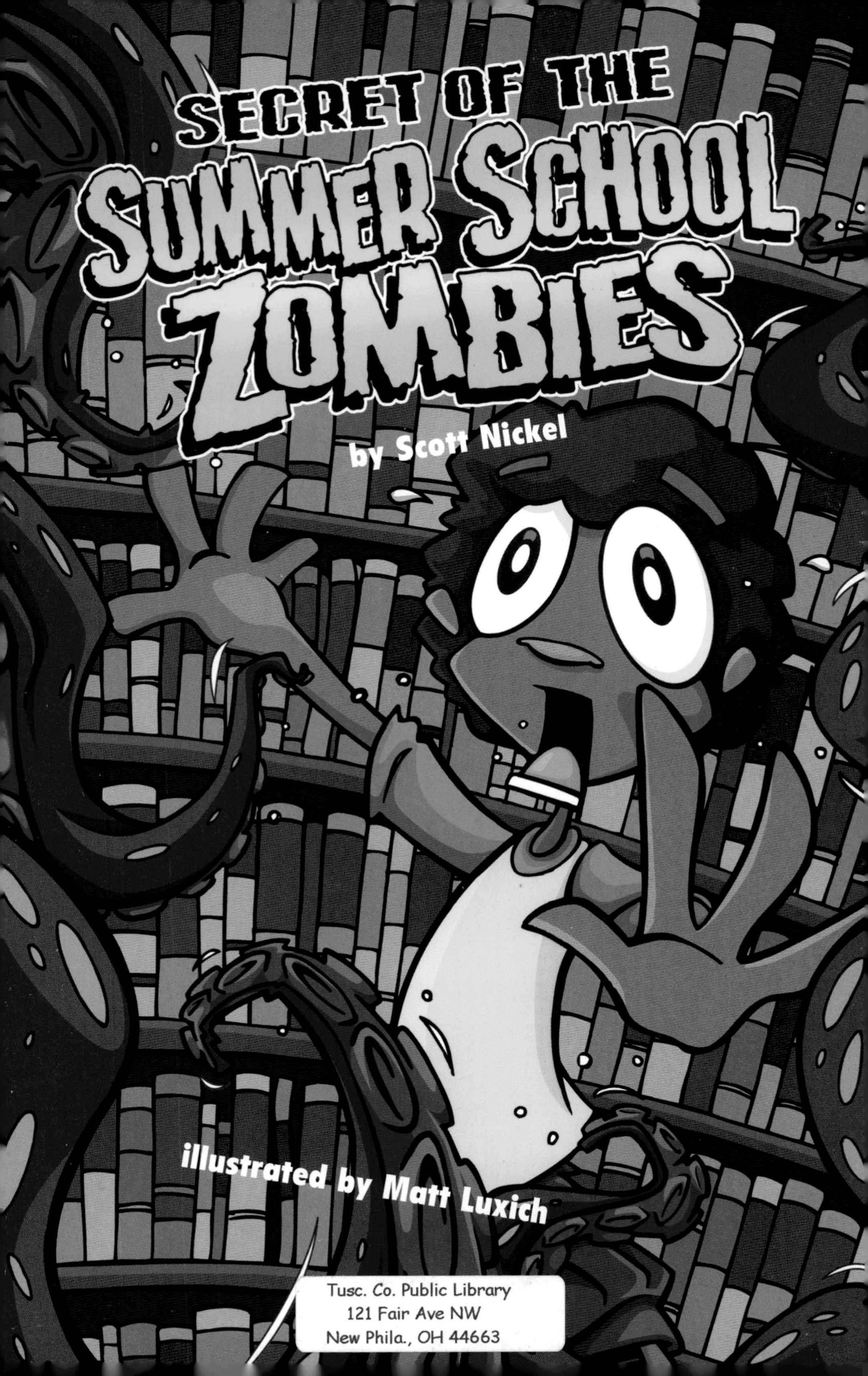
SECRET OF THE
SUMMER SCHOOL
ZOMBIES
by Scott Nickel
illustrated by Matt Luxich

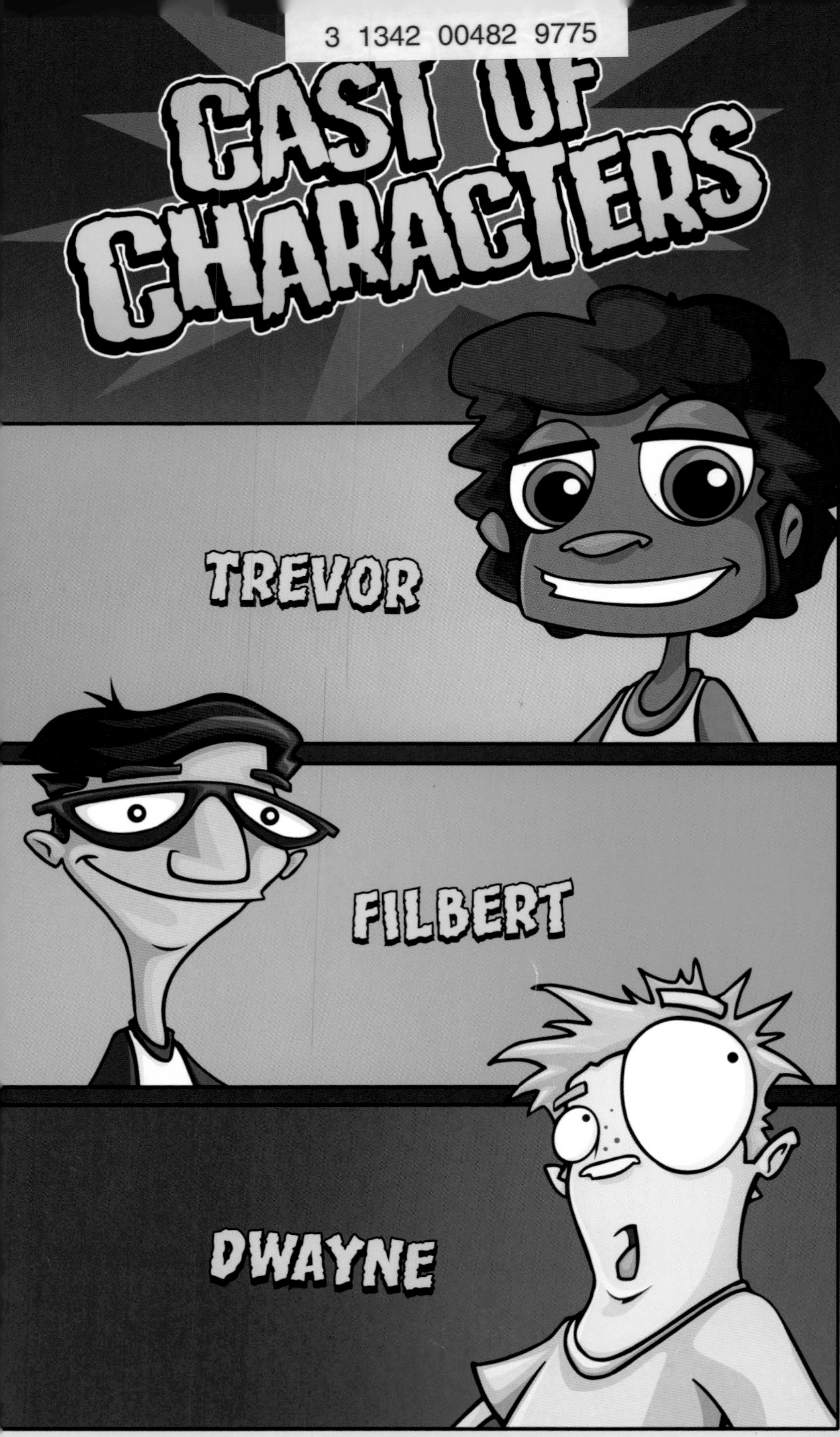
CAST OF CHARACTERS
TREVOR
FILBERT
DWAYNE

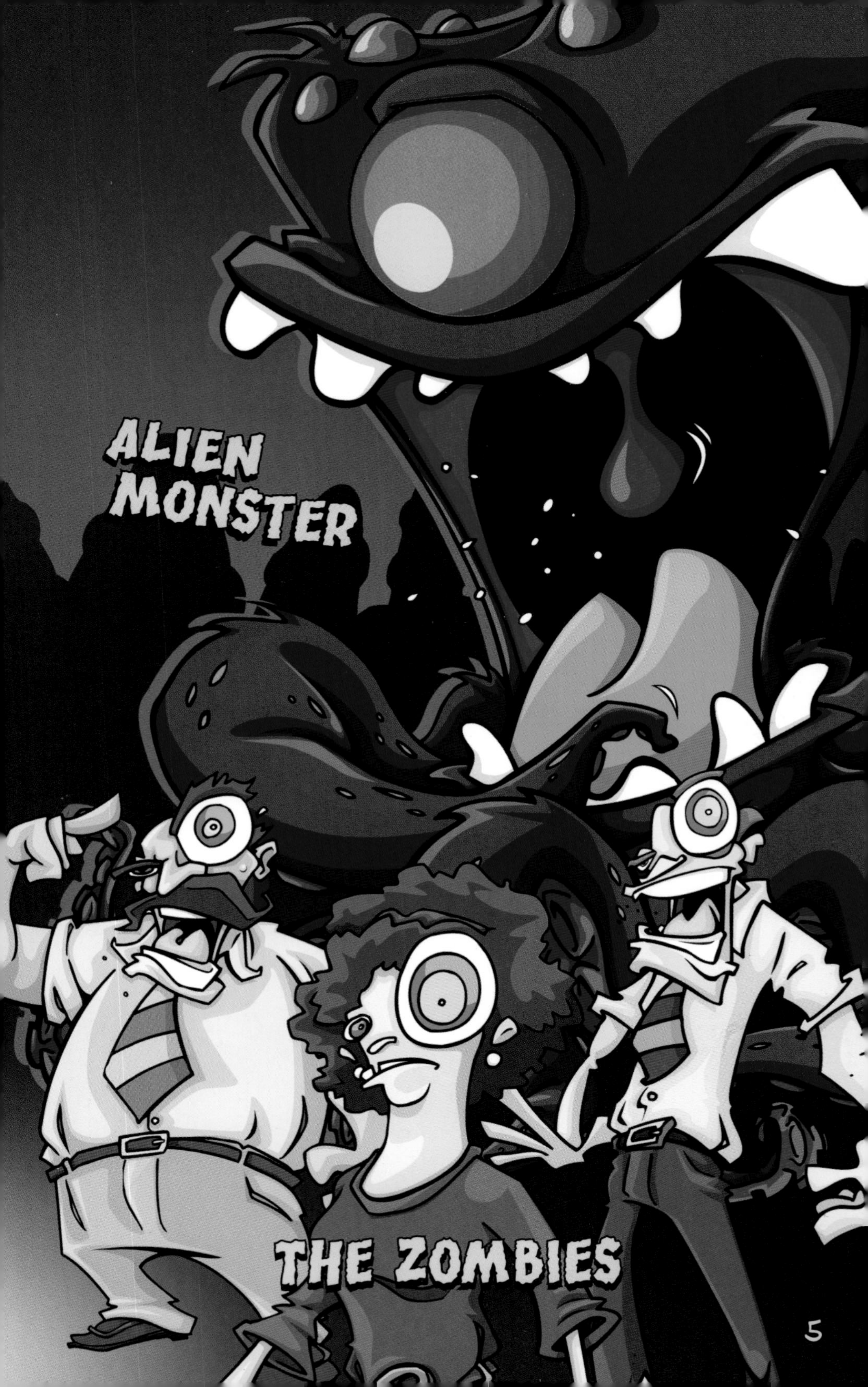
ALIEN MONSTER
THE ZOMBIES

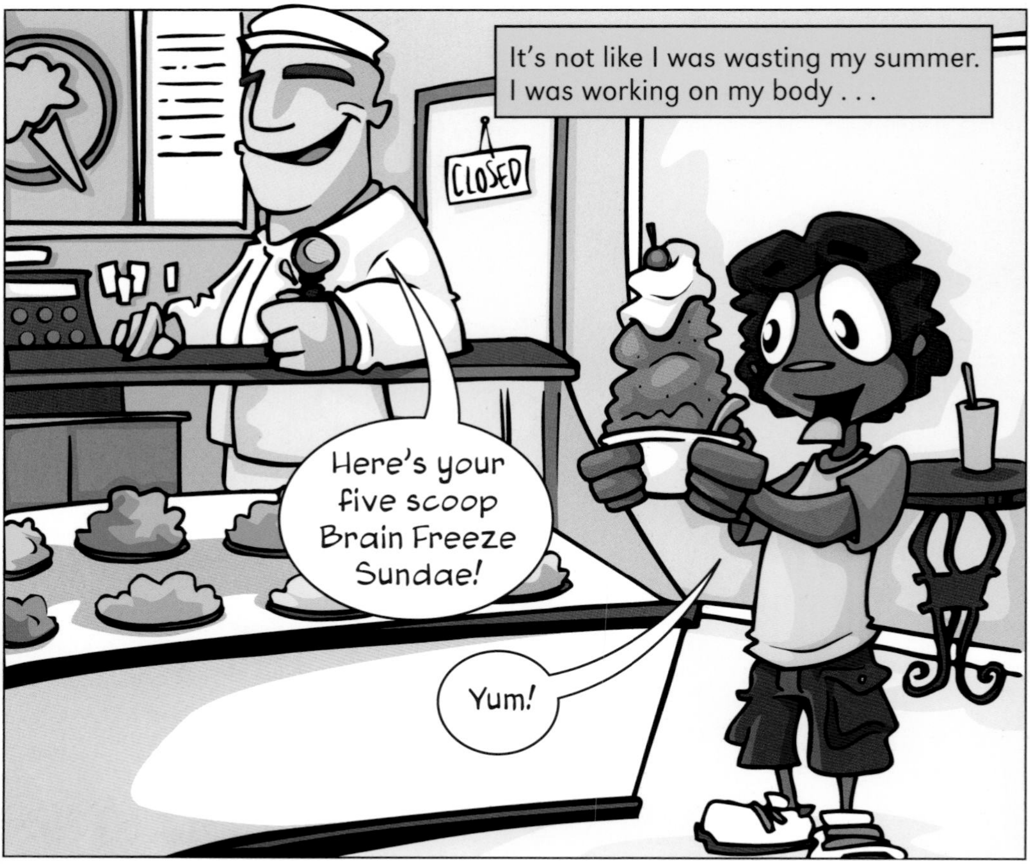
It's not like I was wasting my summer. I was working on my body . . .
CLOSED
Here's your five scoop Brain Freeze Sundae!
Yum!

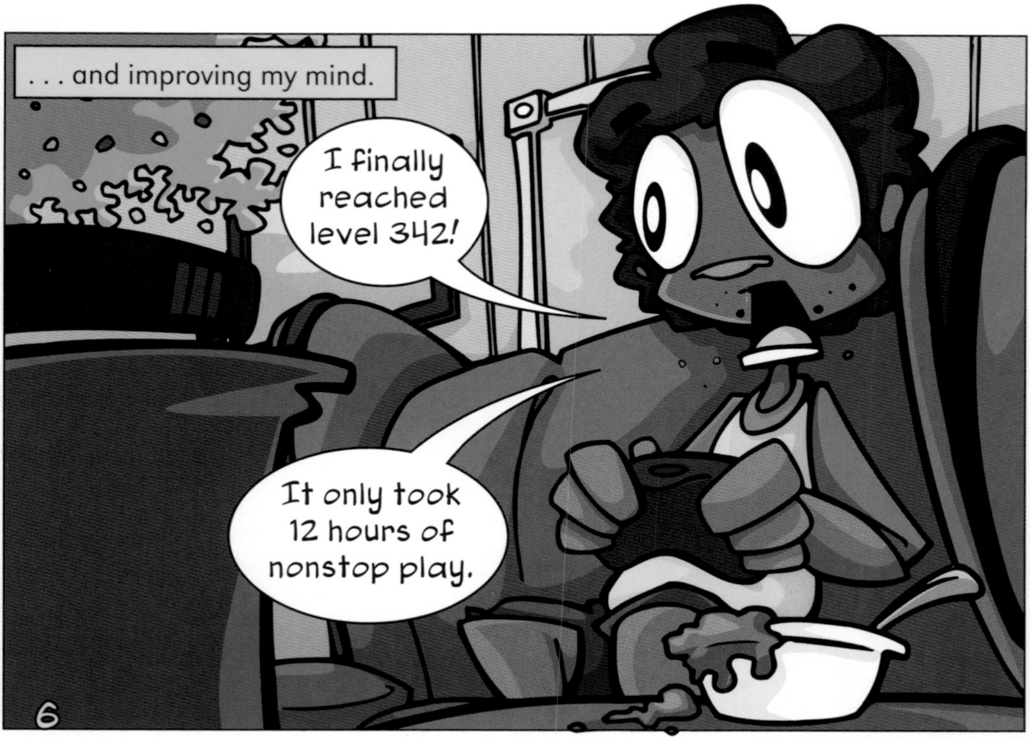
. . . and improving my mind.
I finally reached level 342!
It only took 12 hours of nonstop play.

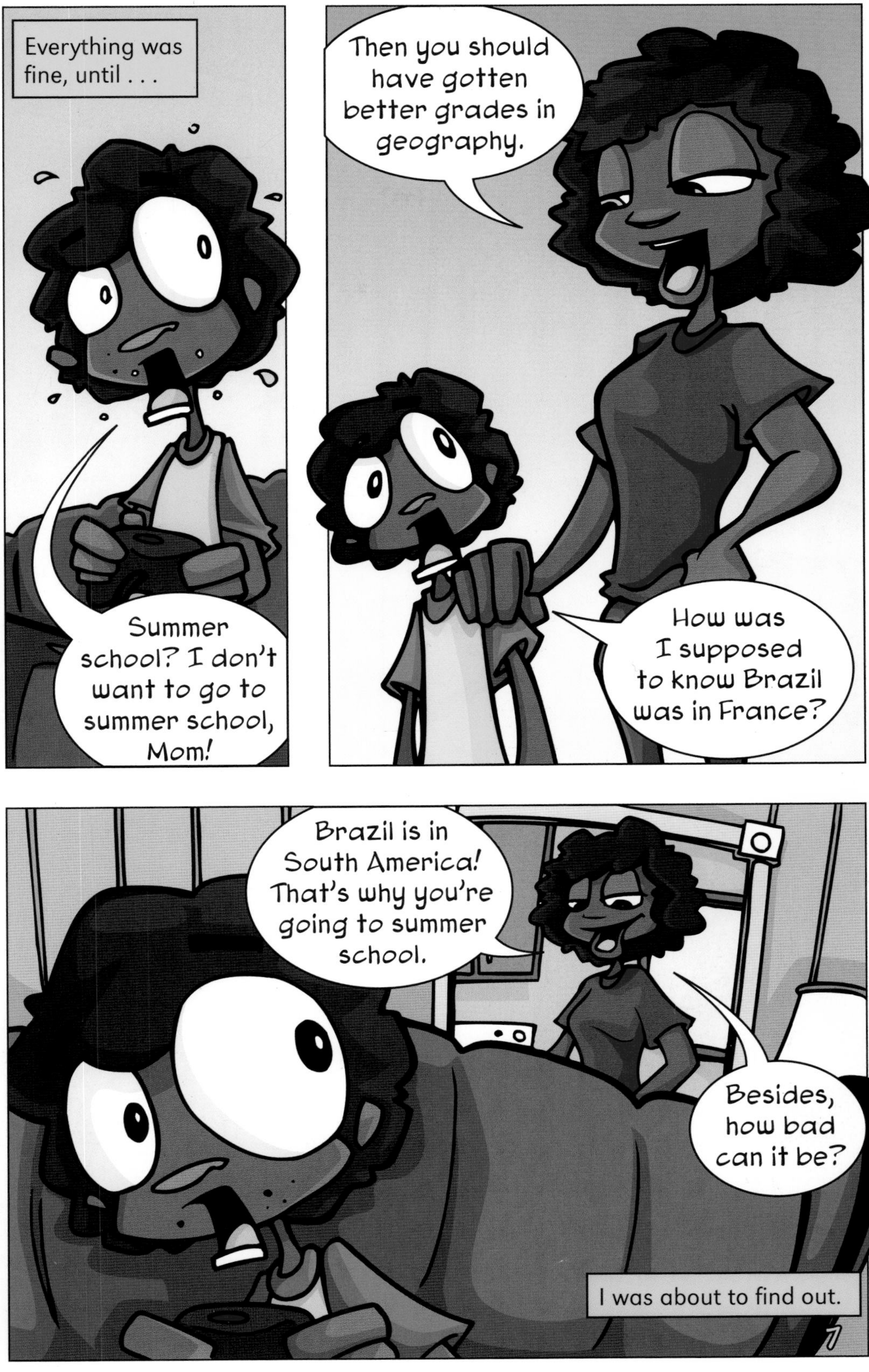

Everything was fine, until . . .
Summer school? I don't want to go to summer school, Mom!
Then you should have gotten better grades in geography.
How was I supposed to know Brazil was in France?
Brazil is in South America! That's why you're going to summer school.
Besides, how bad can it be?
I was about to find out.

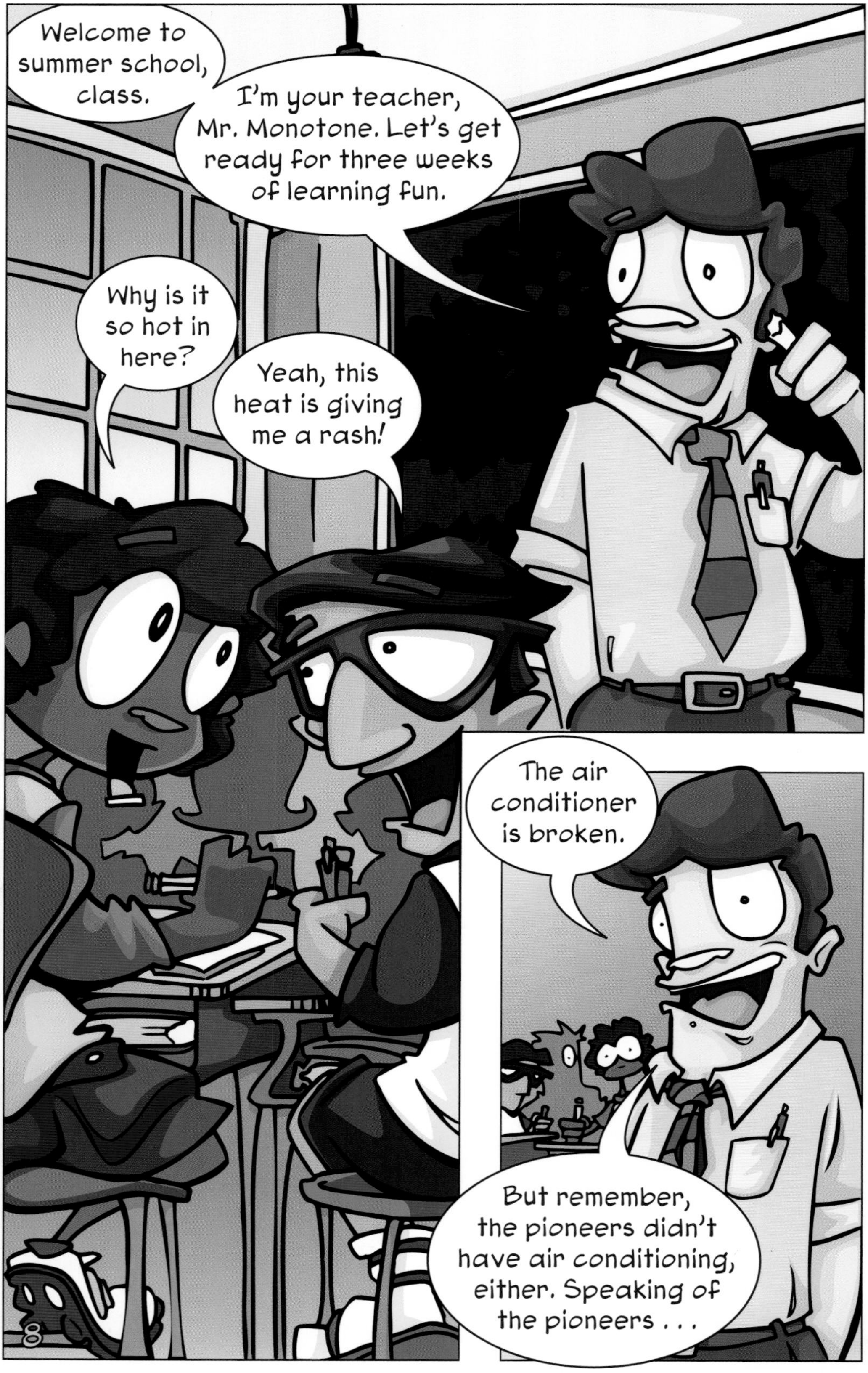
Welcome to summer school, class.
I'm your teacher, Mr. Monotone. Let's get ready for three weeks of learning fun.
Why is it so hot in here?
Yeah, this heat is giving me a rash!
The air conditioner is broken.
But remember, the pioneers didn't have air conditioning, either. Speaking of the pioneers . . .

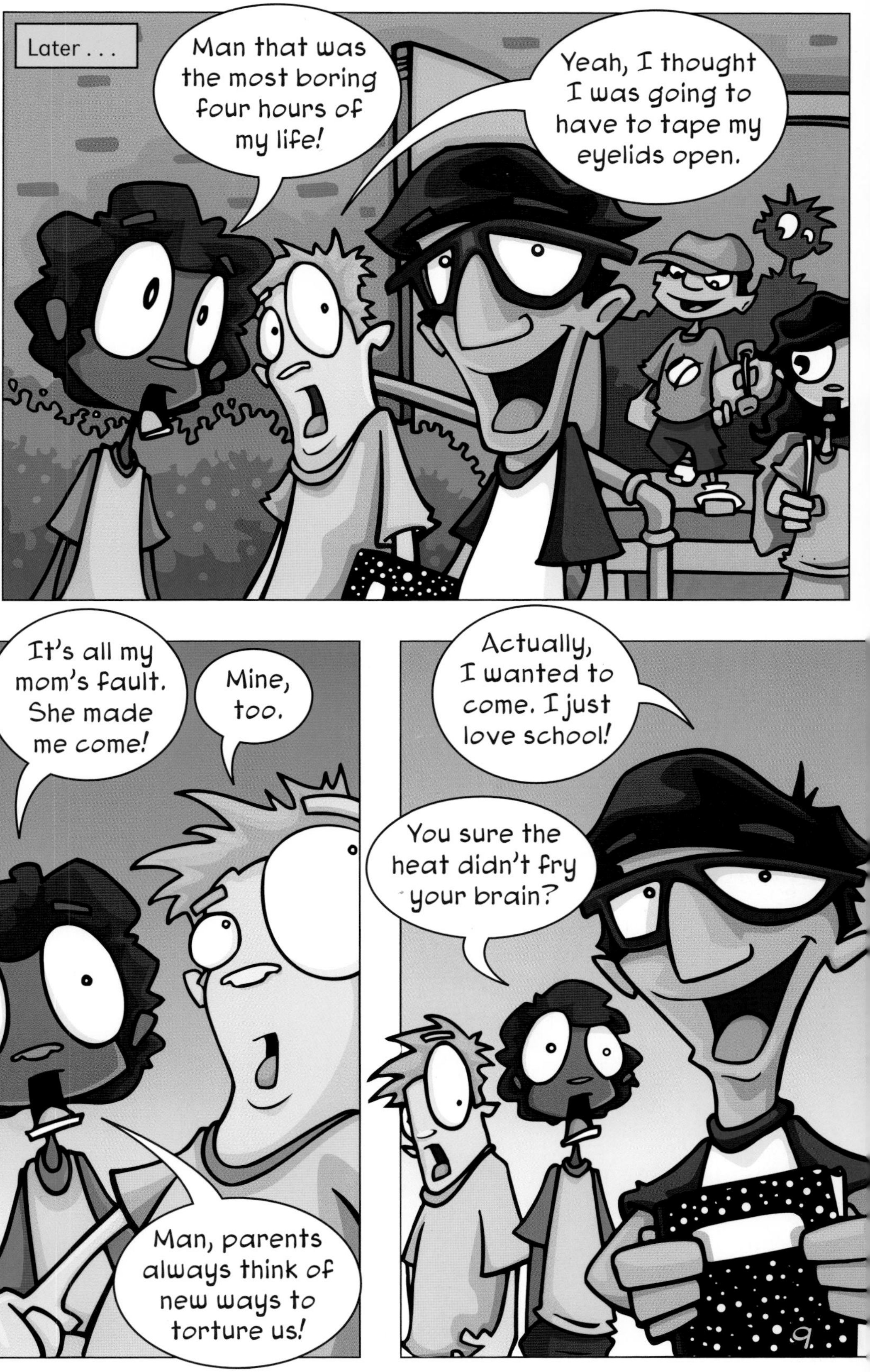
Later . . .
Man that was the most boring four hours of my life!
Yeah, I thought I was going to have to tape my eyelids open.
It's all my mom's fault. She made me come!
Mine, too.
Man, parents always think of new ways to torture us!
Actually, I wanted to come. I just love school!
You sure the heat didn't fry your brain?

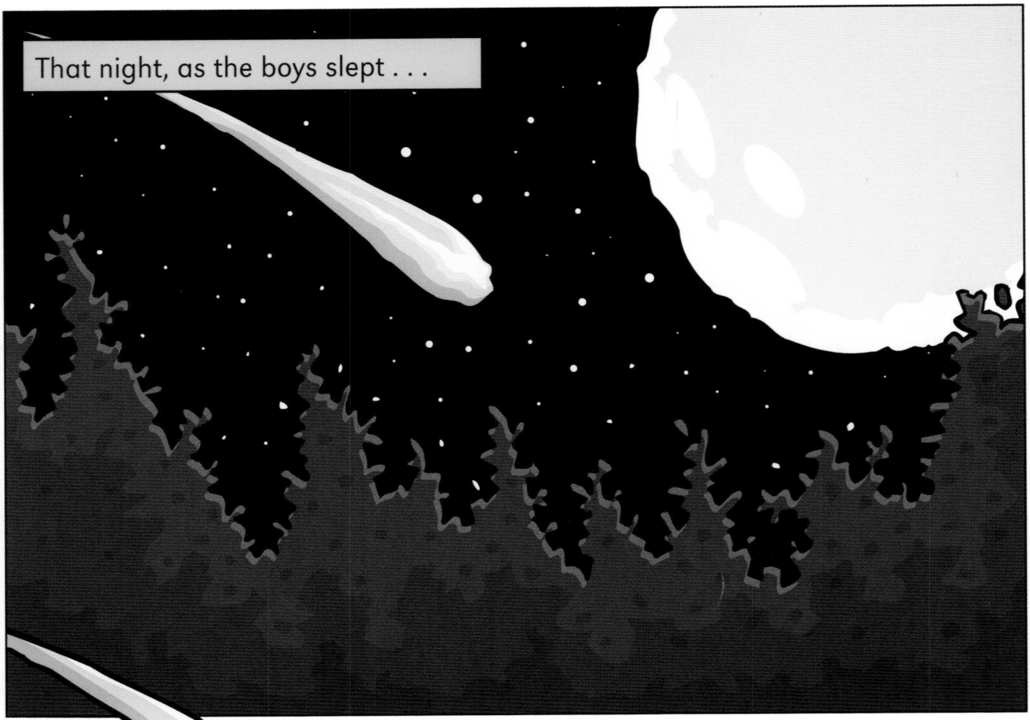
That night, as the boys slept . . .

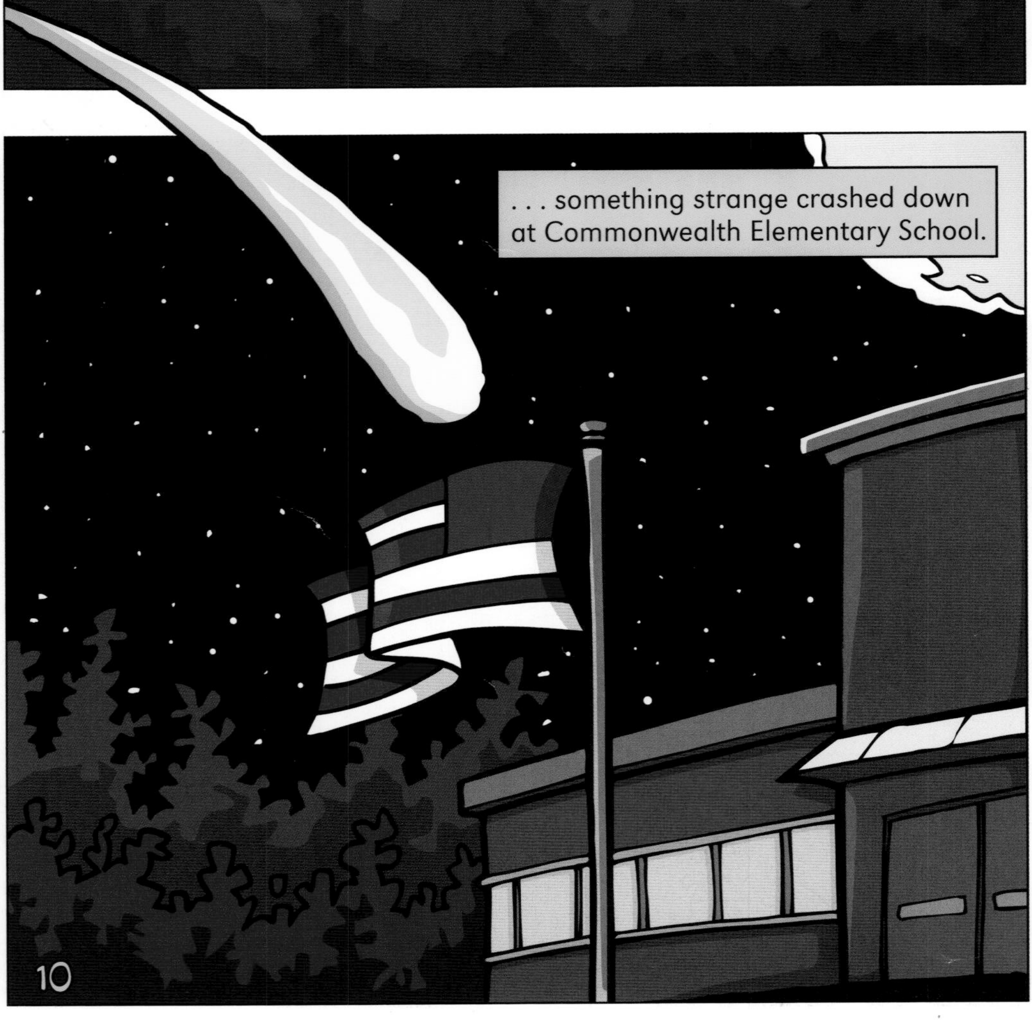
. . . something strange crashed down at Commonwealth Elementary School.

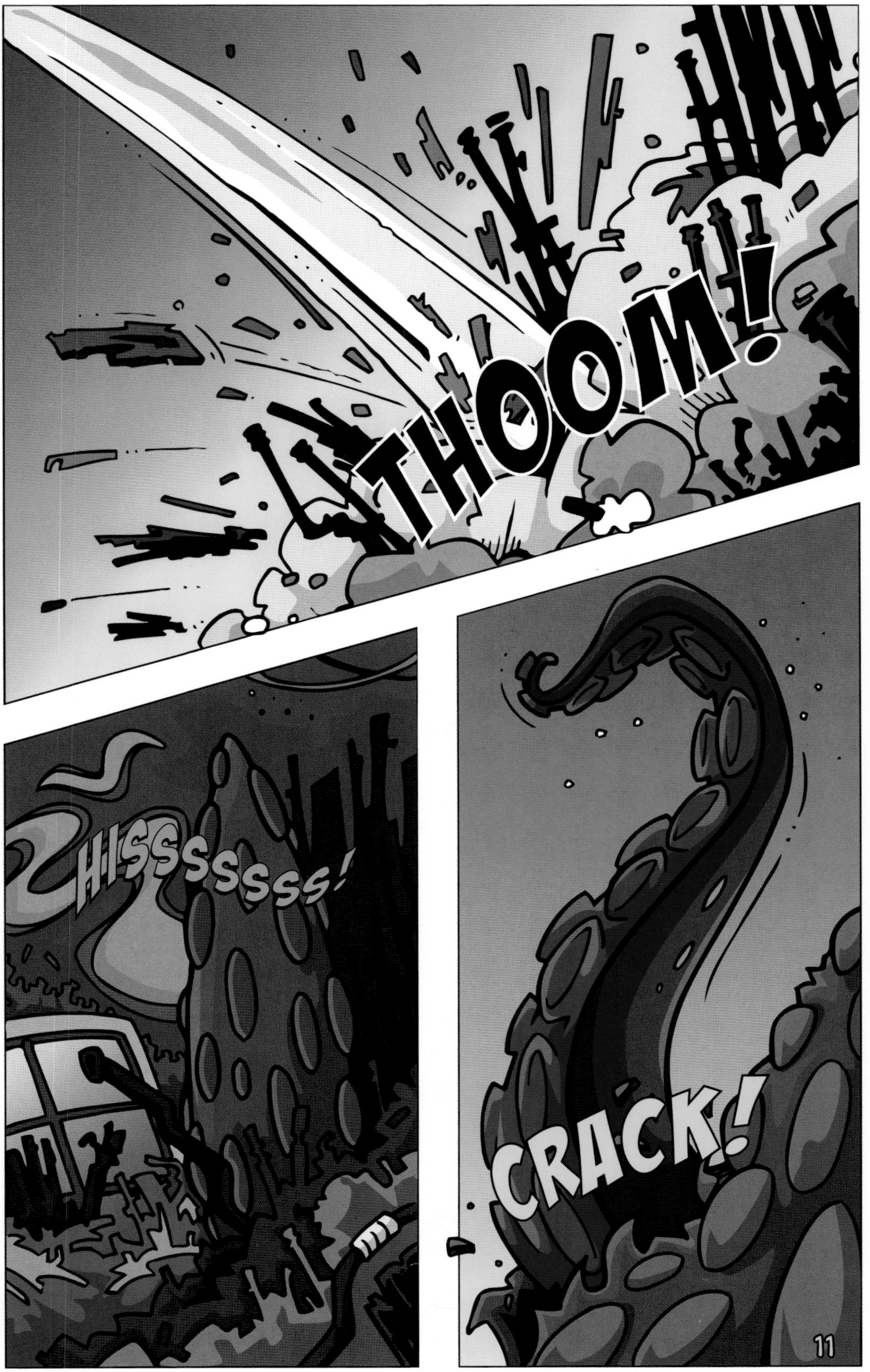
THOOM!
HISSSSSSS!
CRACK!

The next day at summer school, Mr. Monotone was acting weird.
Must give pop quiz! Must give pop quiz!
What's wrong with Mr. Monotone?
I think he's turned into some kind of creepy summer school zombie!
Just then the door burst open!

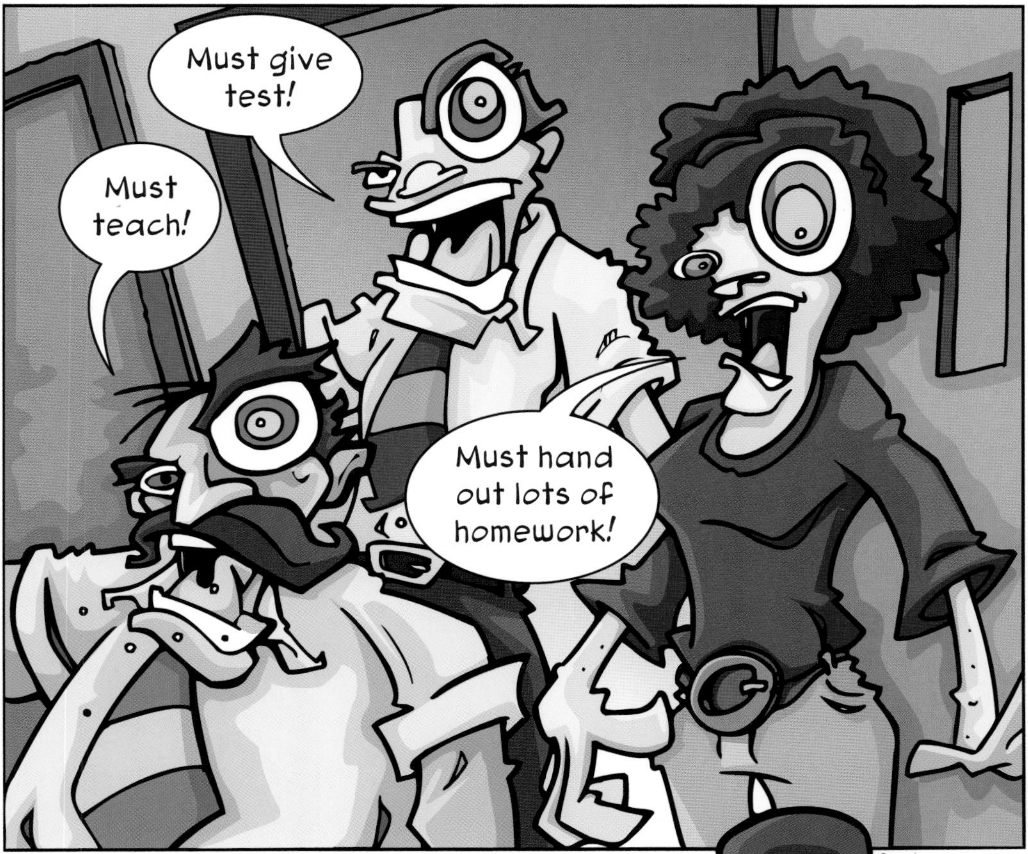
Must teach!
Must give test!
Must hand out lots of homework!

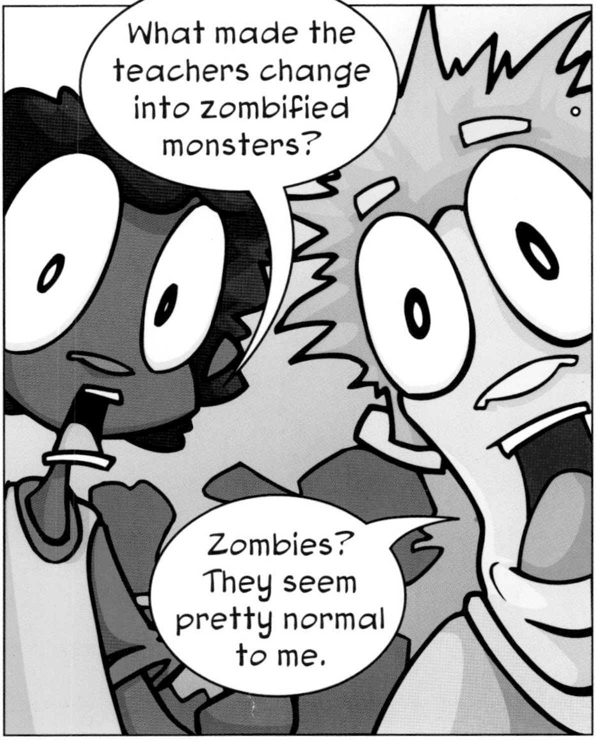
What made the teachers change into zombified monsters?
Zombies? They seem pretty normal to me.

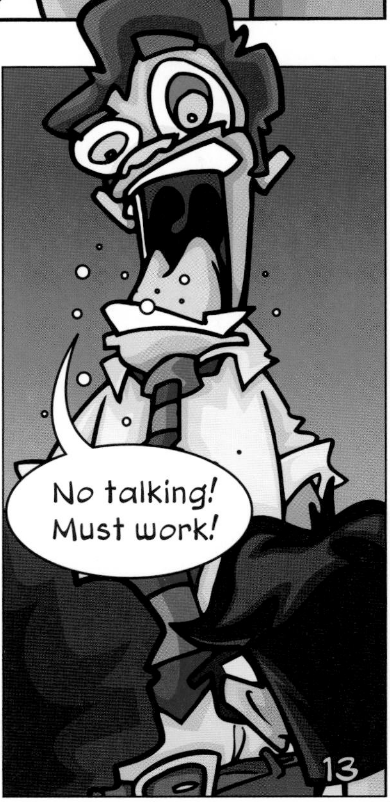
No talking! Must work!

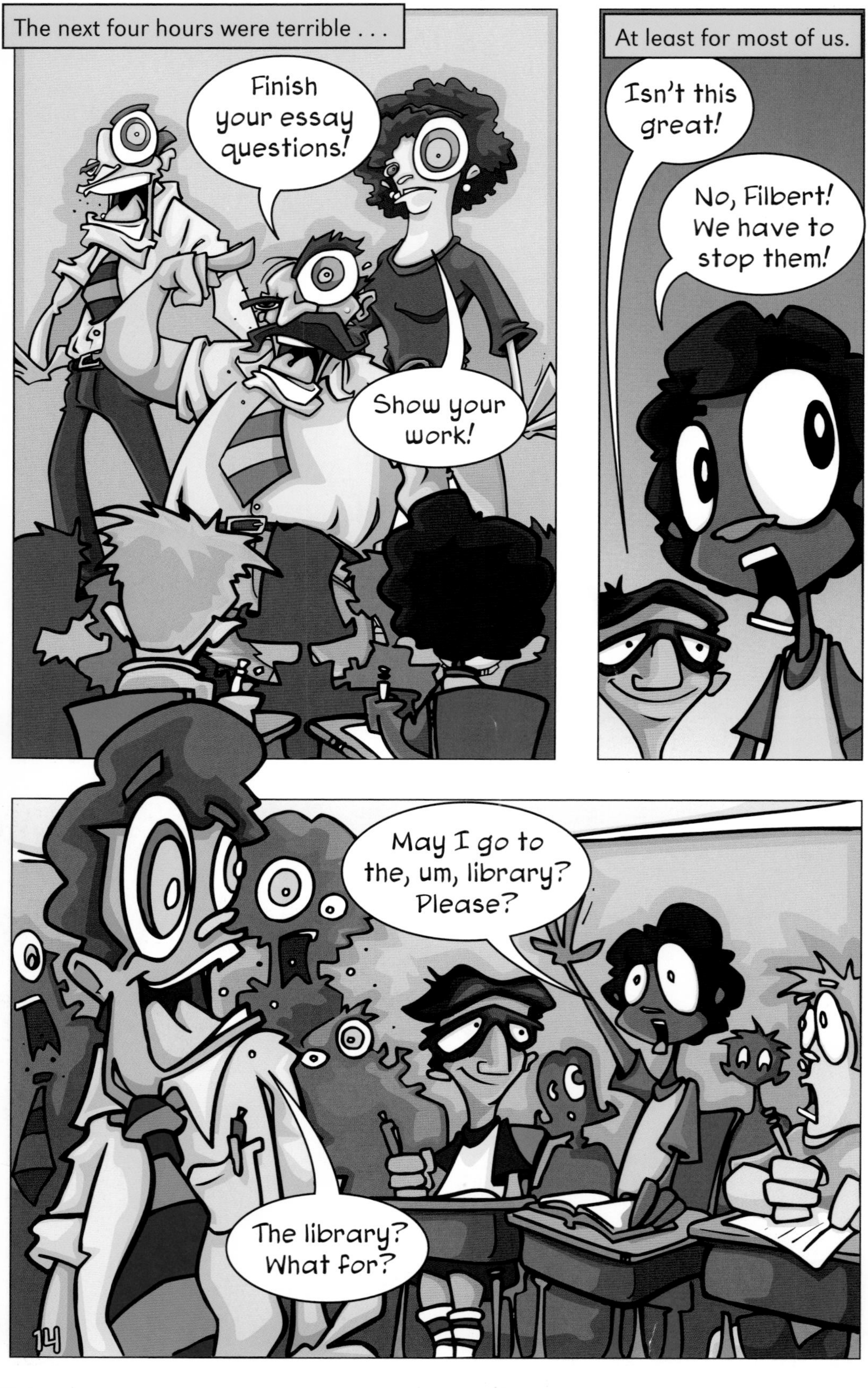
The next four hours were terrible . . .
Finish your essay questions!
Show your work!
At least for most of us.
Isn't this great!
No, Filbert! We have to stop them!
May I go to the, um, library? Please?
The library? What for?

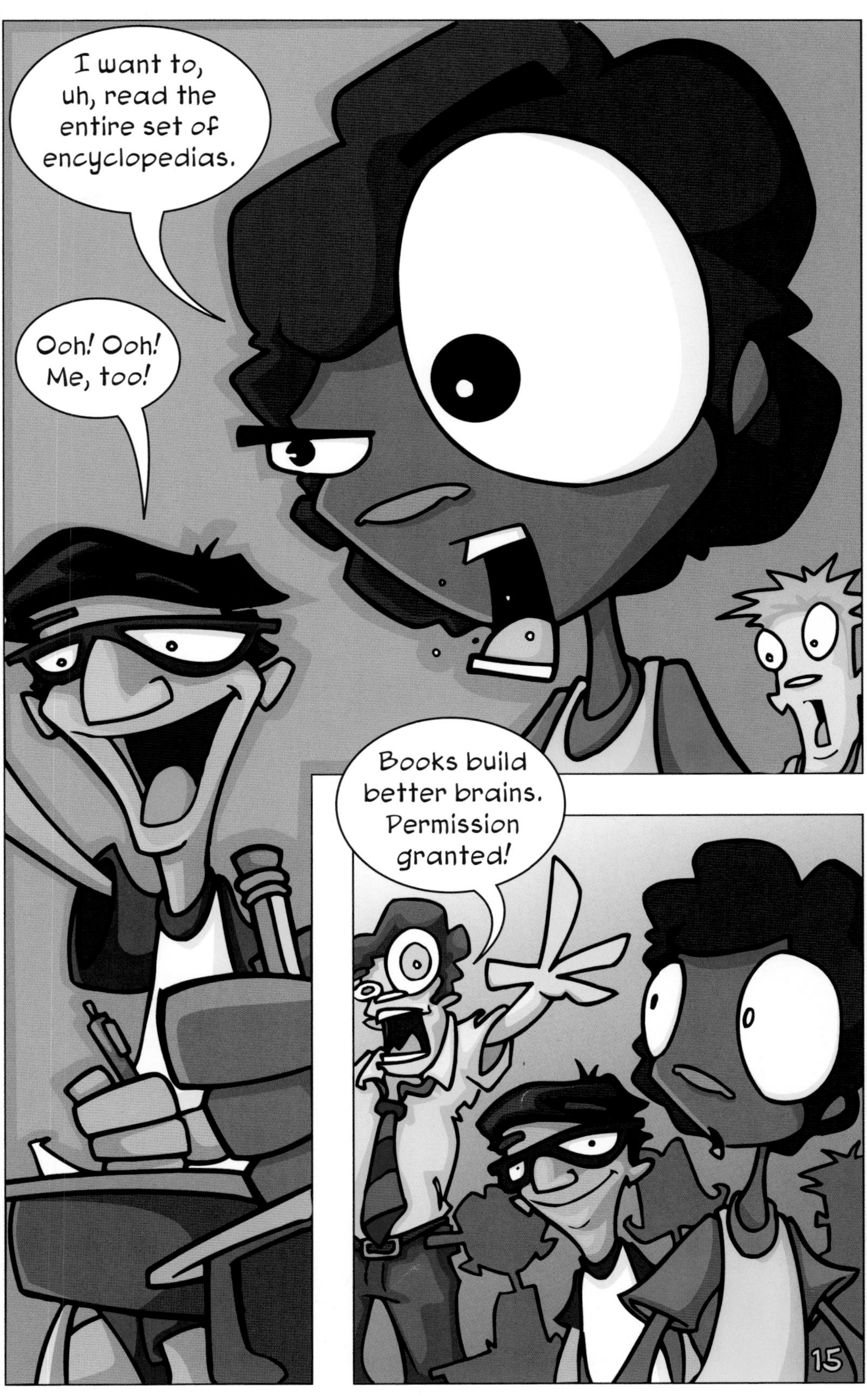

I want to, uh, read the entire set of encyclopedias.
Ooh! Ooh! Me, too!
Books build better brains. Permission granted!

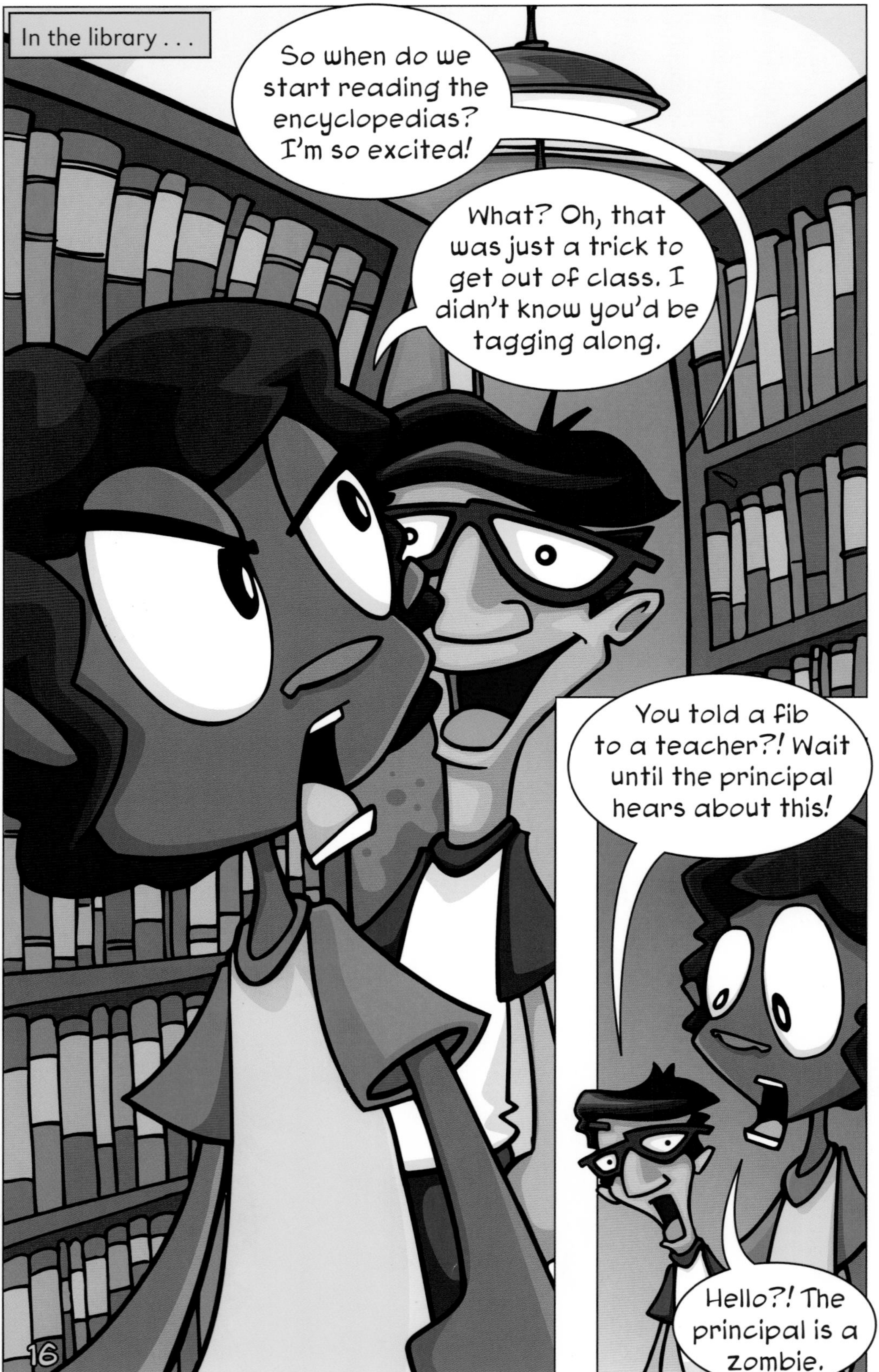
In the library . . .
So when do we start reading the encyclopedias? I'm so excited!
What? Oh, that was just a trick to get out of class. I didn't know you'd be tagging along.
You told a fib to a teacher?! Wait until the principal hears about this!
Hello?! The principal is a zombie.

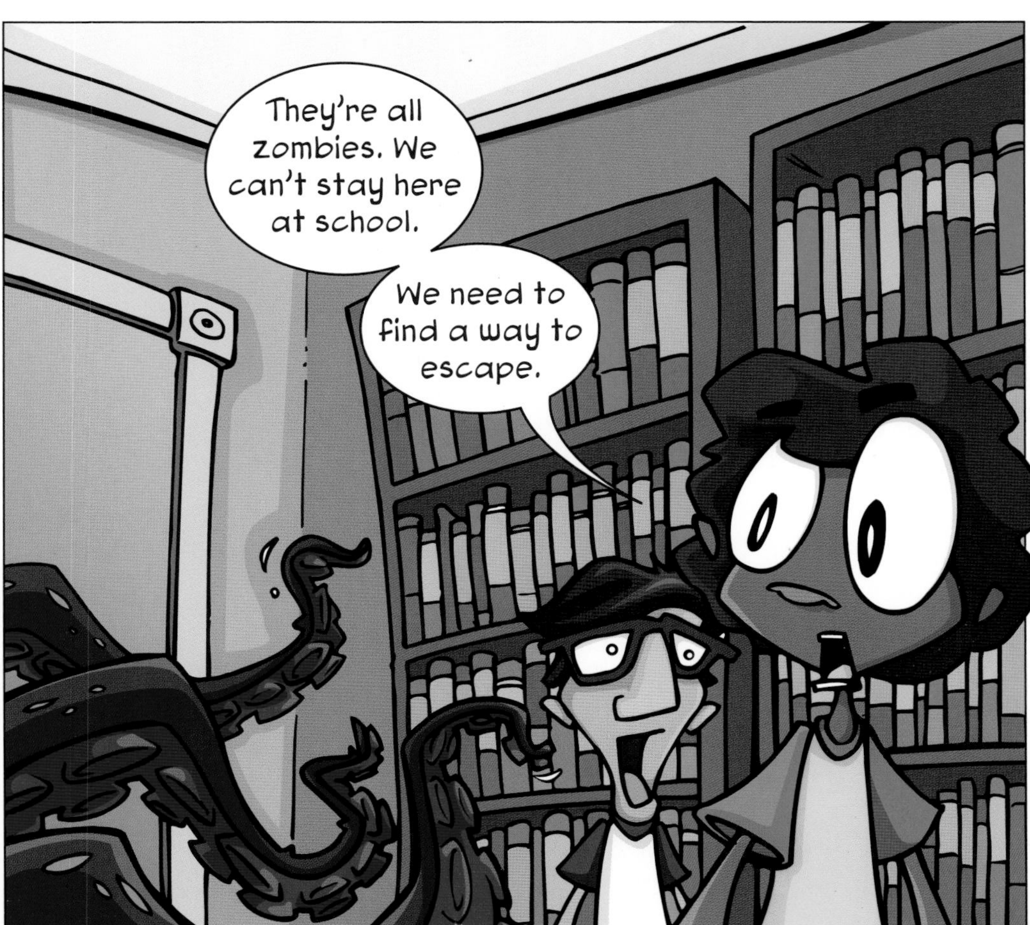
They're all zombies. We can't stay here at school.
We need to find a way to escape.

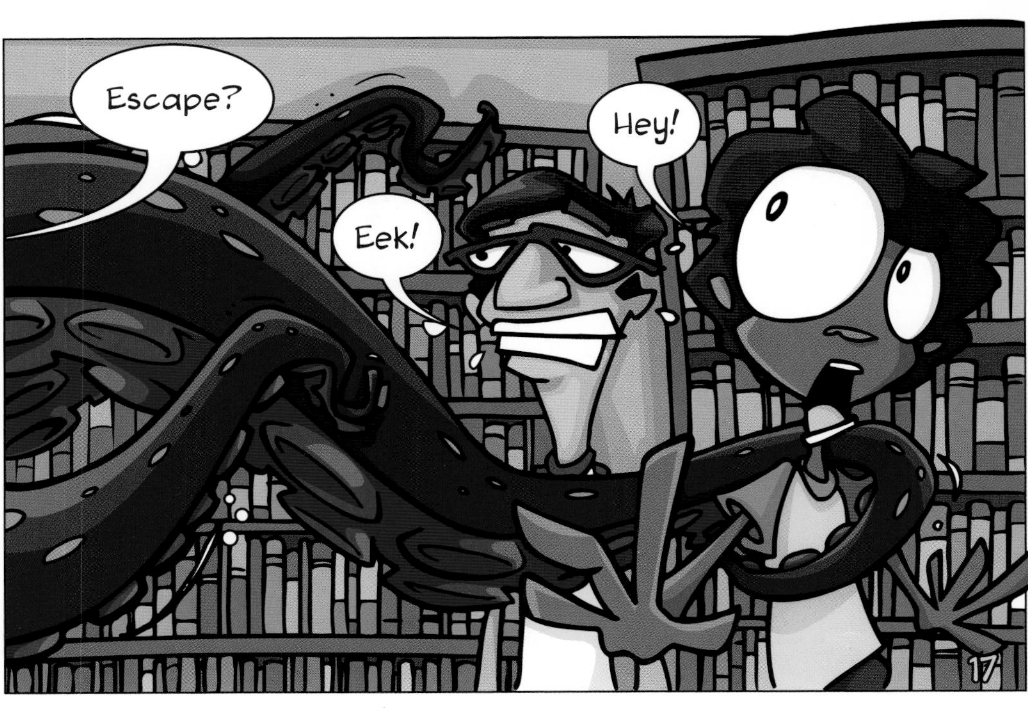
Escape?
Hey!
Eek!

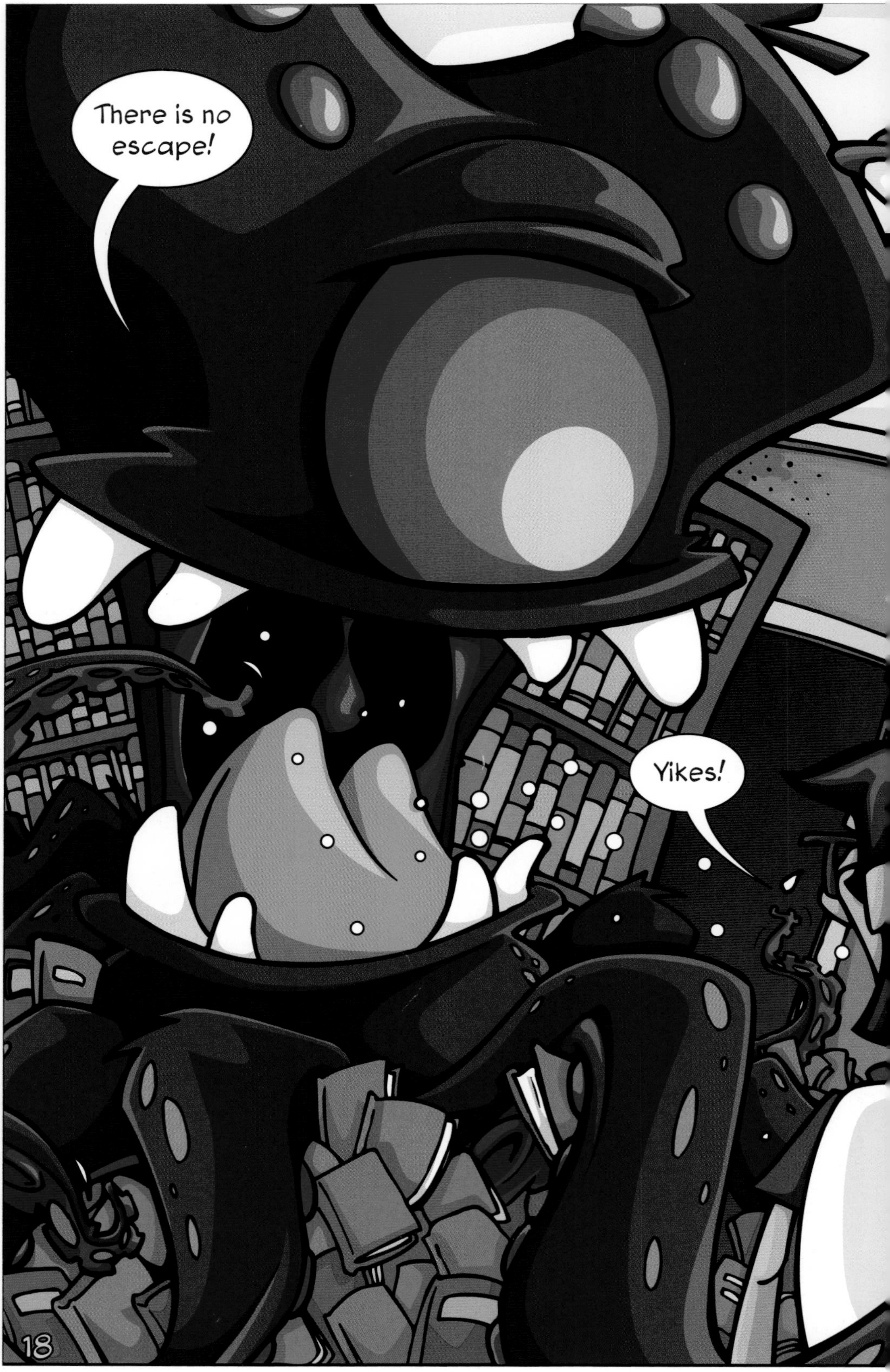
There is no escape!
Yikes!

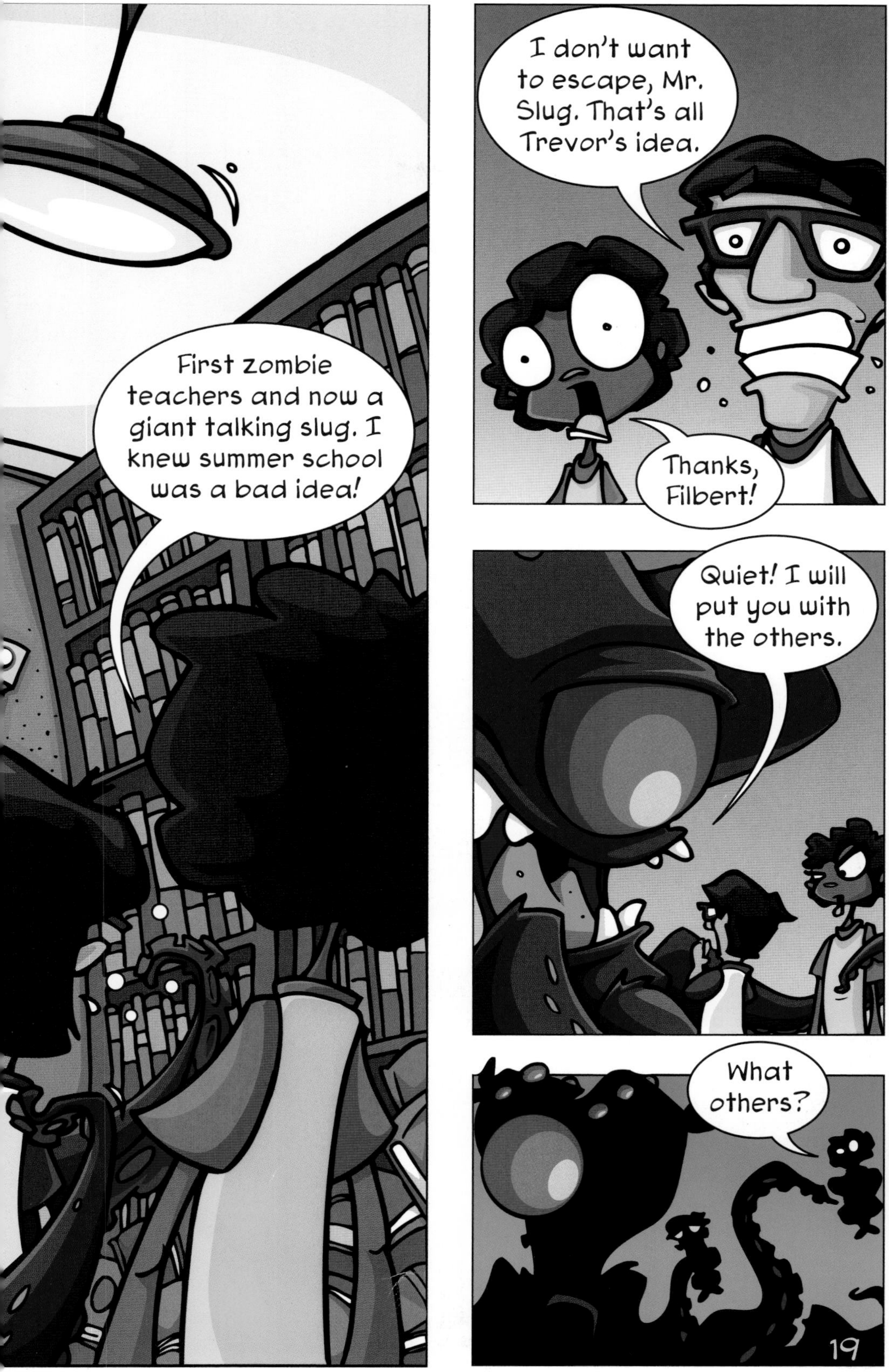

First zombie teachers and now a giant talking slug. I knew summer school was a bad idea!
I don't want to escape, Mr. Slug. That's all Trevor's idea.
Thanks, Filbert!
Quiet! I will put you with the others.
What others?

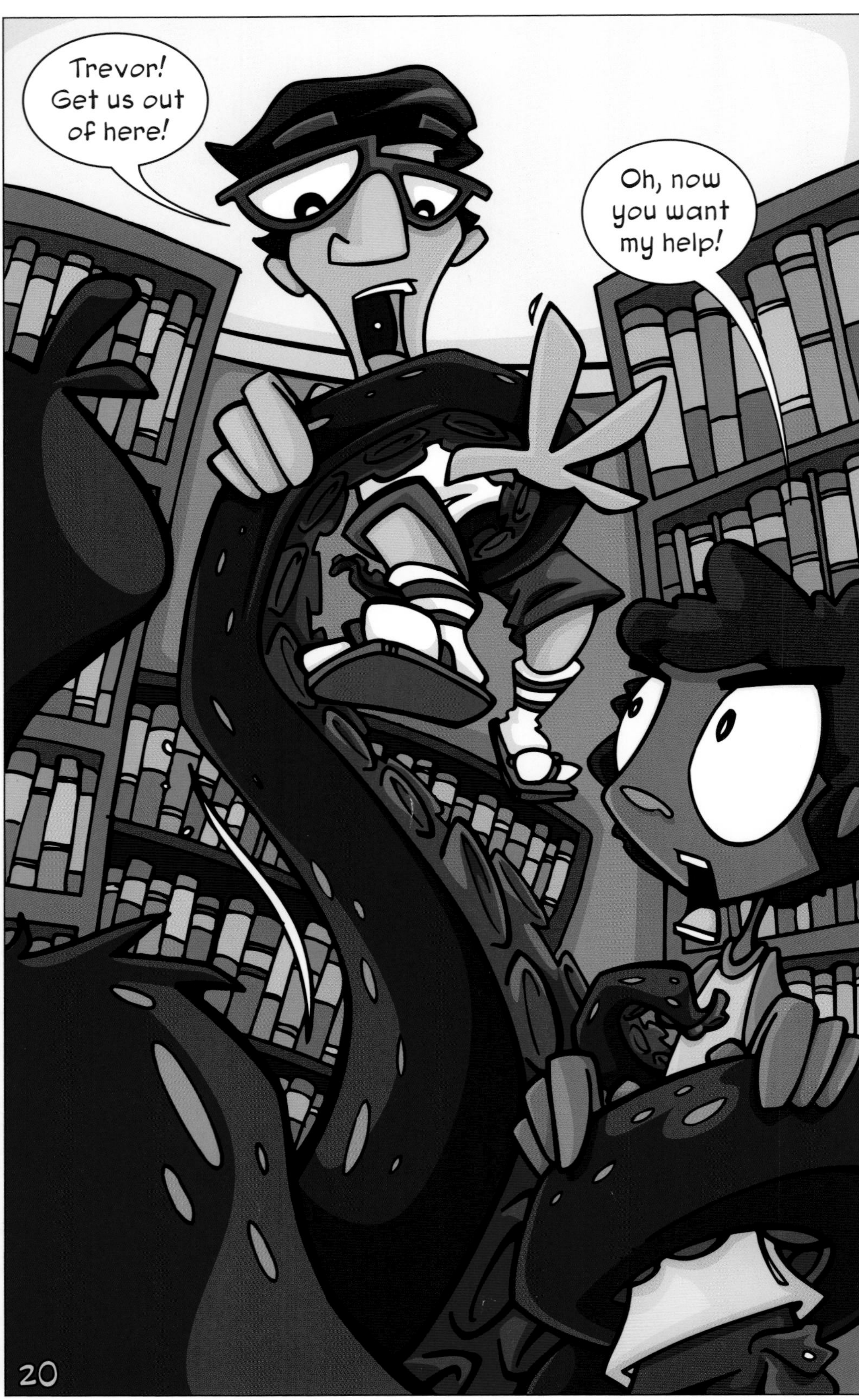
Trevor! Get us out of here!
Oh, now you want my help!

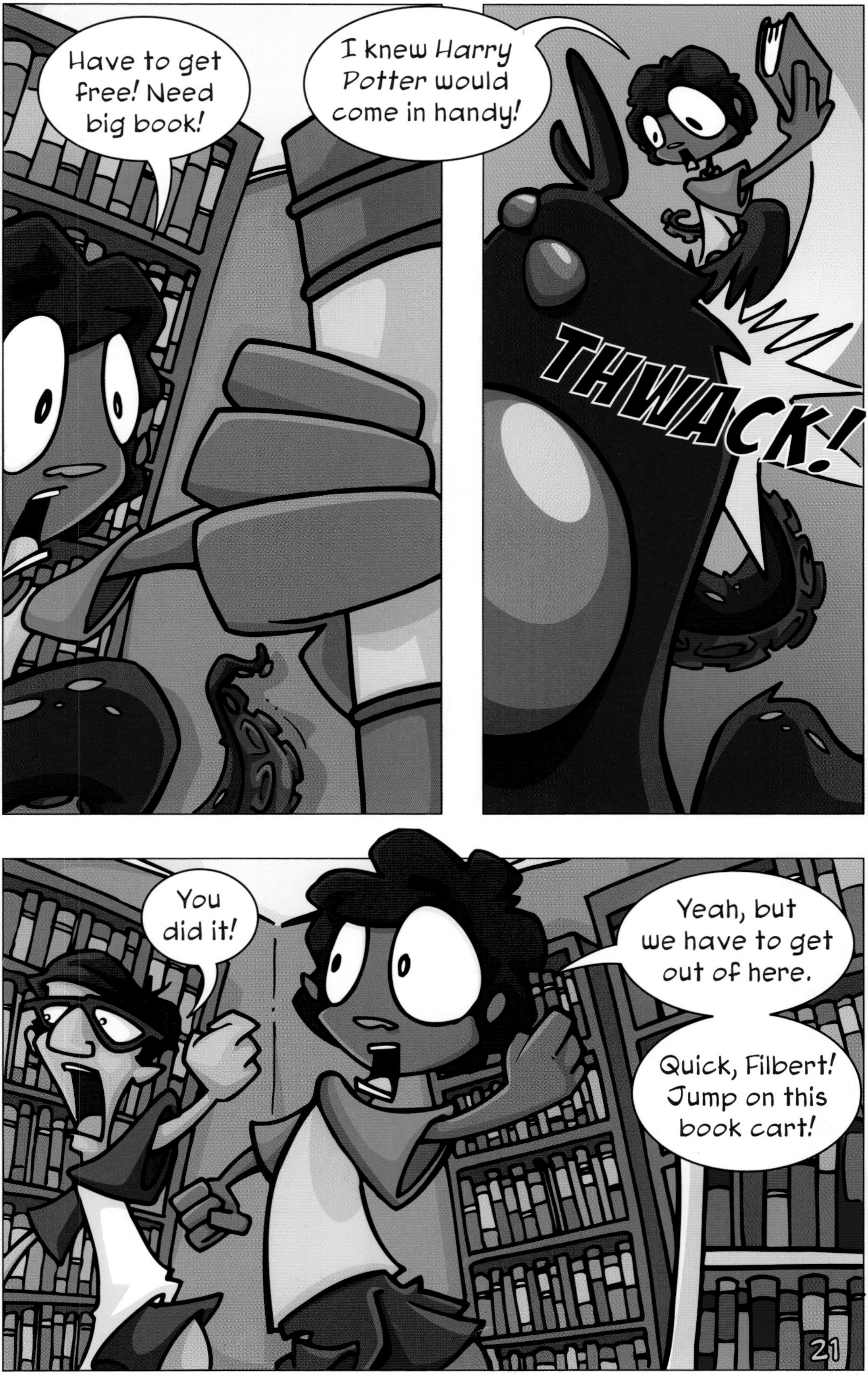
Have to get free! Need big book!
I knew *Harry Potter* would come in handy!
THWACK!
You did it!
Yeah, but we have to get out of here.
Quick, Filbert! Jump on this book cart!

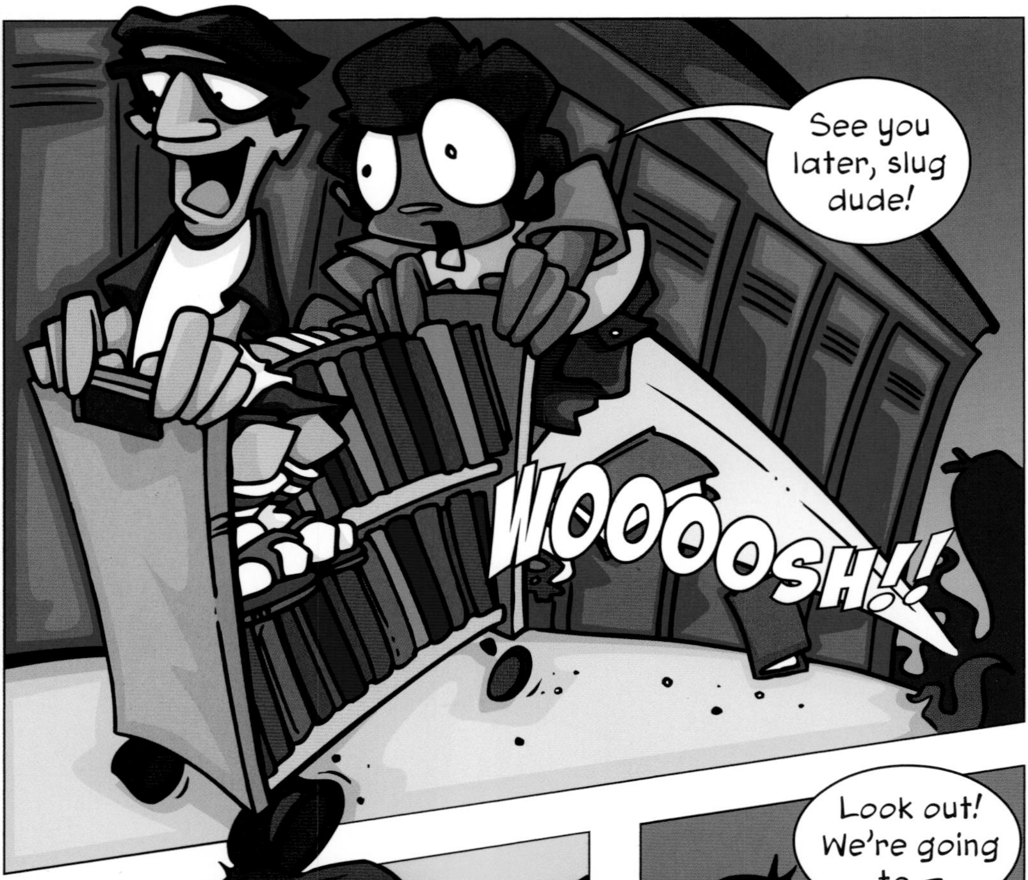

See you later, slug dude!
WOOOOSH!!

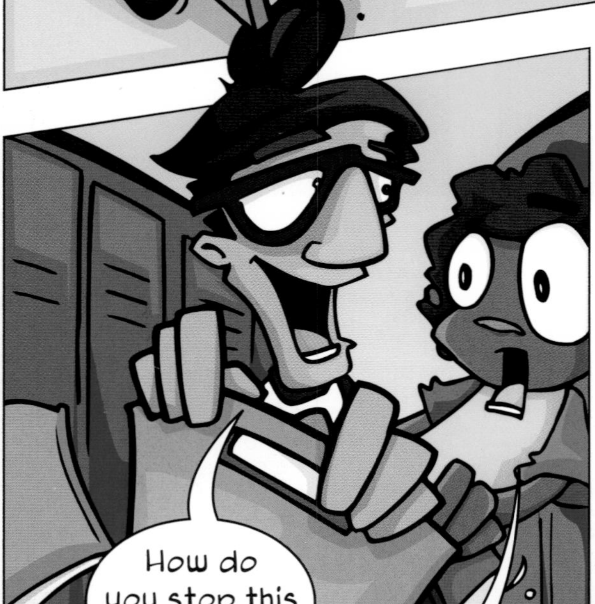

How do you stop this thing?
How should I know! I'm not a librarian!

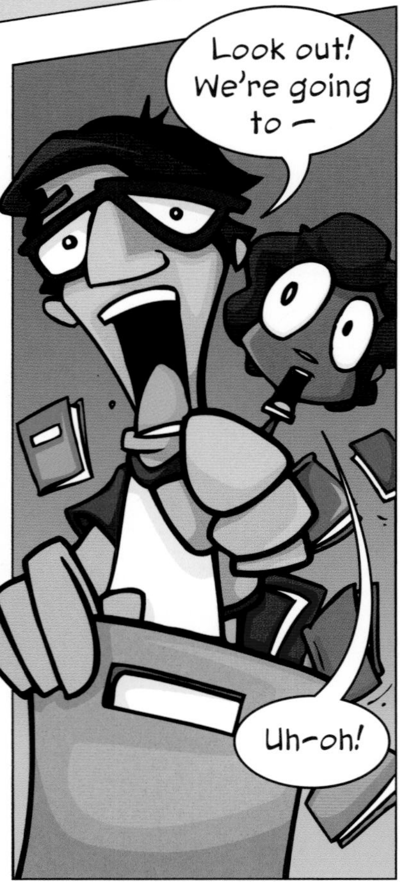

Look out! We're going to —
Uh-oh!

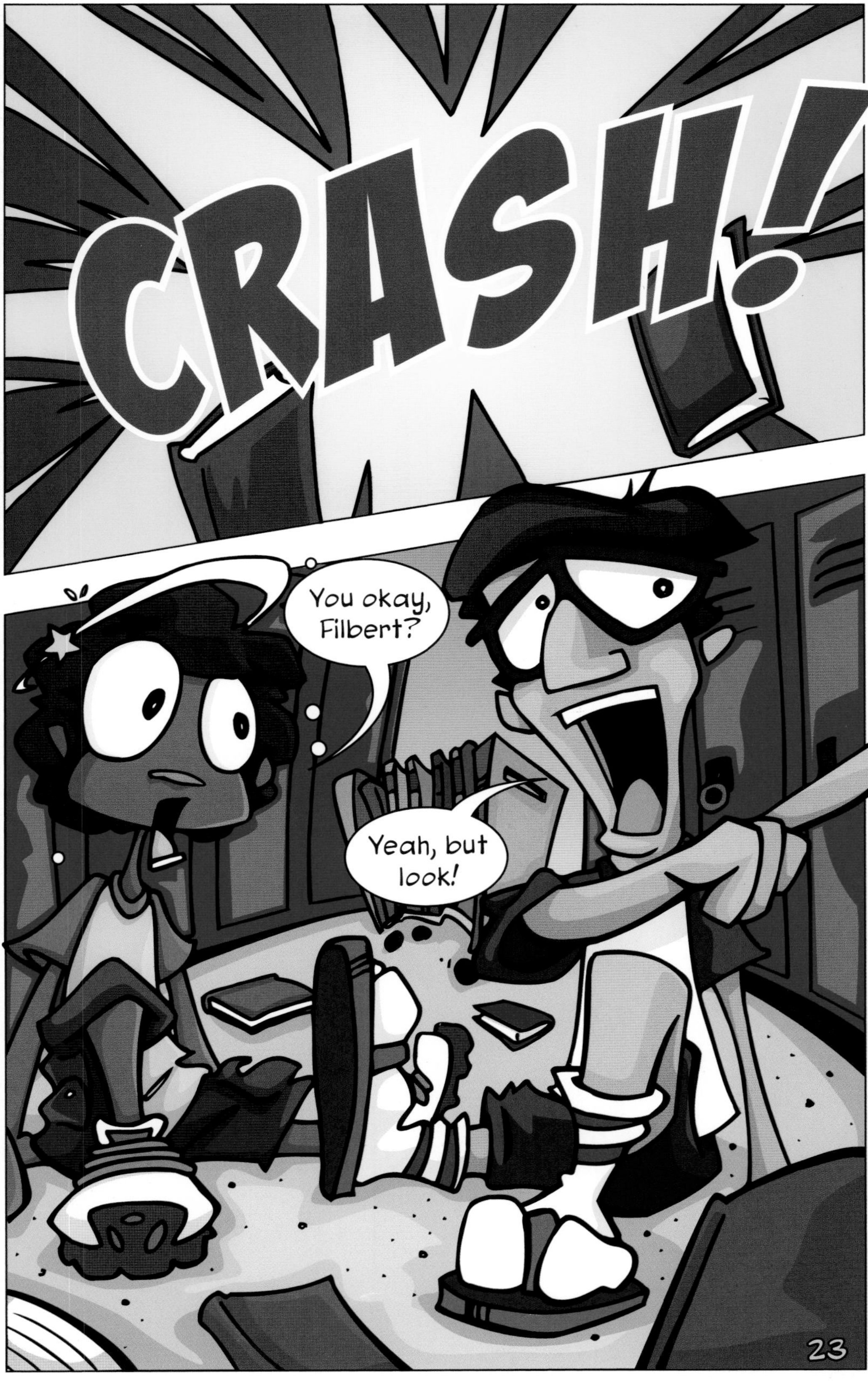
CRASH!
You okay, Filbert?
Yeah, but look!

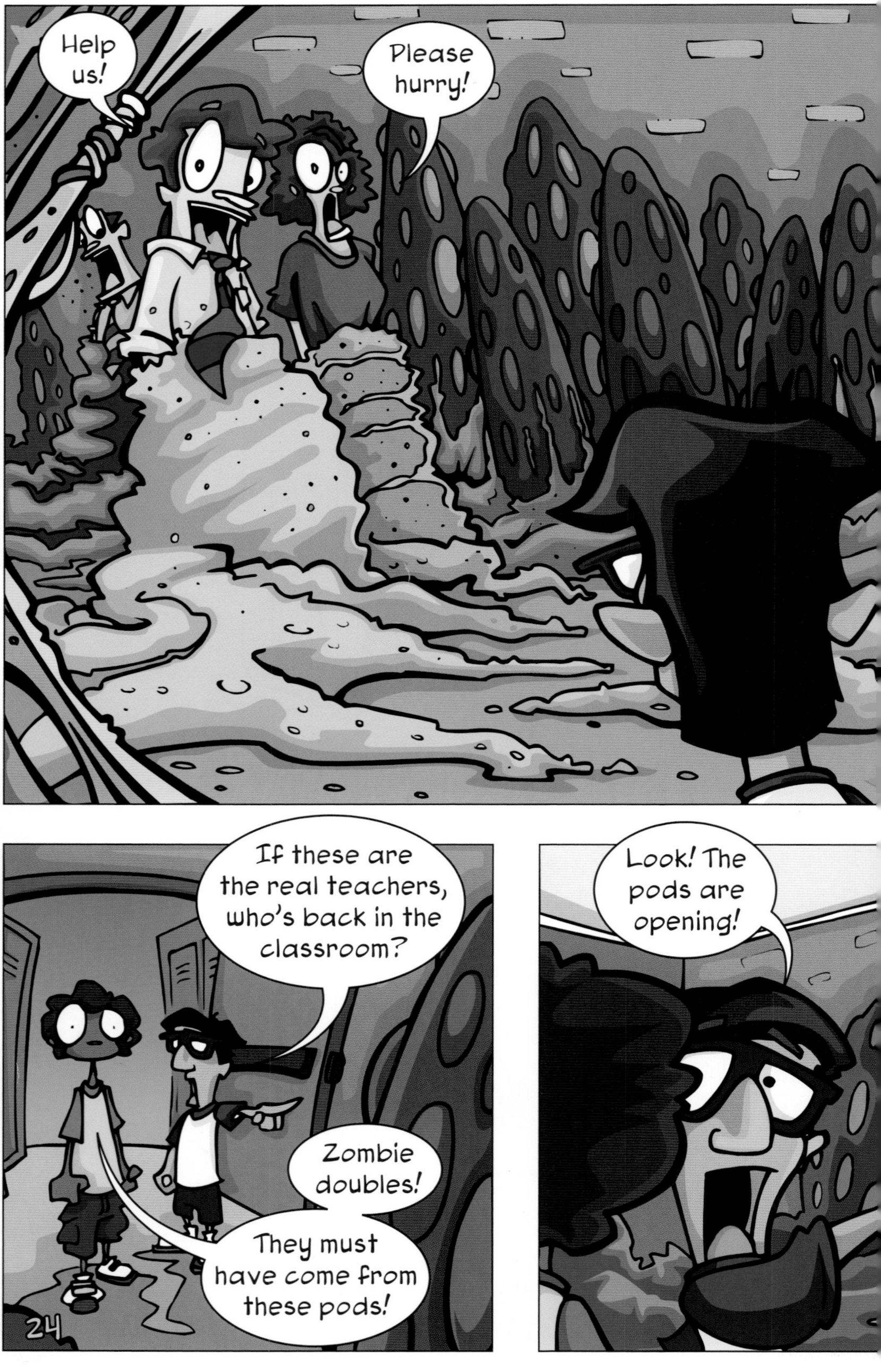
Help us!
Please hurry!
If these are the real teachers, who's back in the classroom?
Zombie doubles!
They must have come from these pods!
Look! The pods are opening!

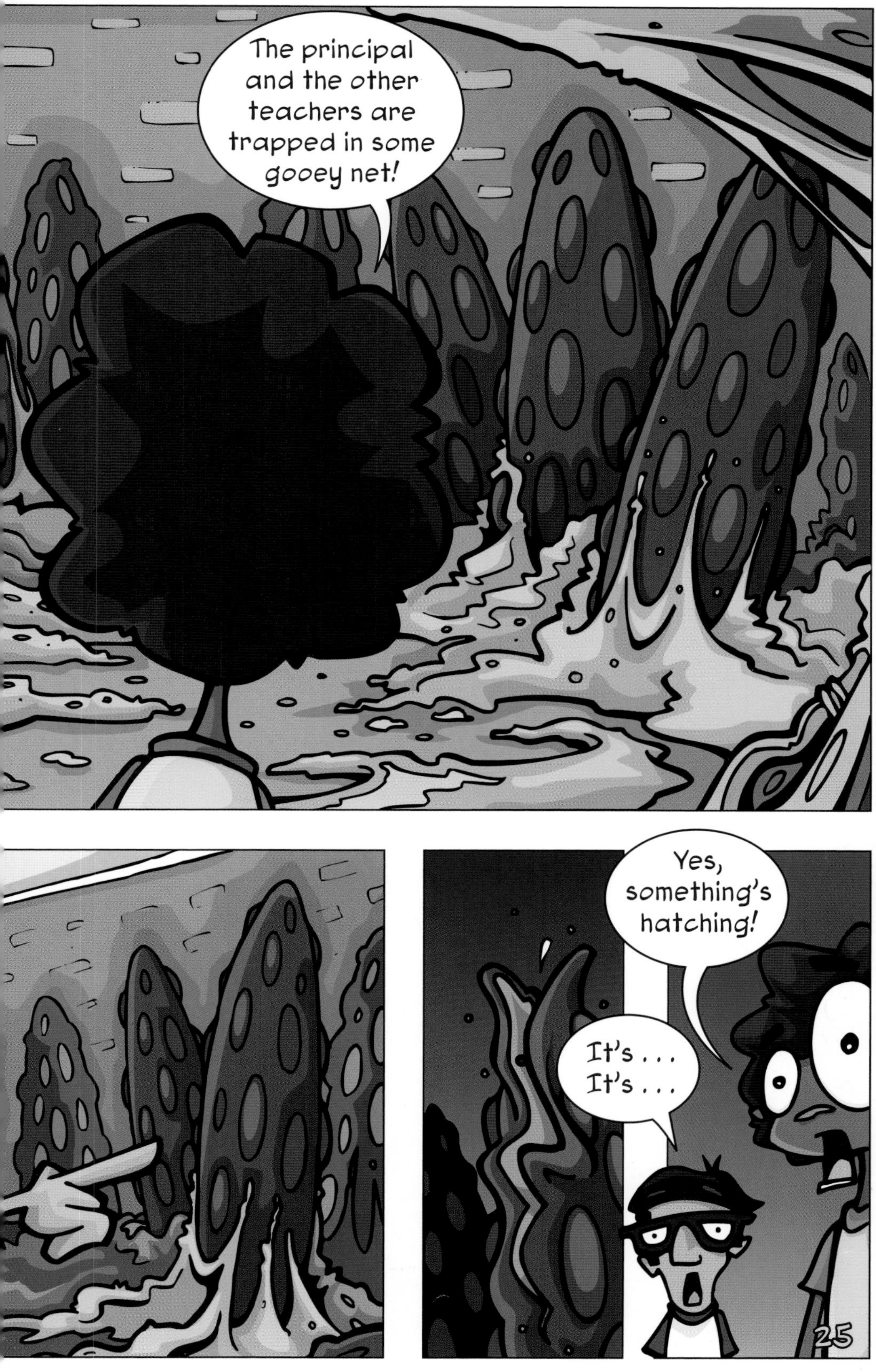
The principal and the other teachers are trapped in some gooey net!
Yes, something's hatching!
It's . . .
It's . . .

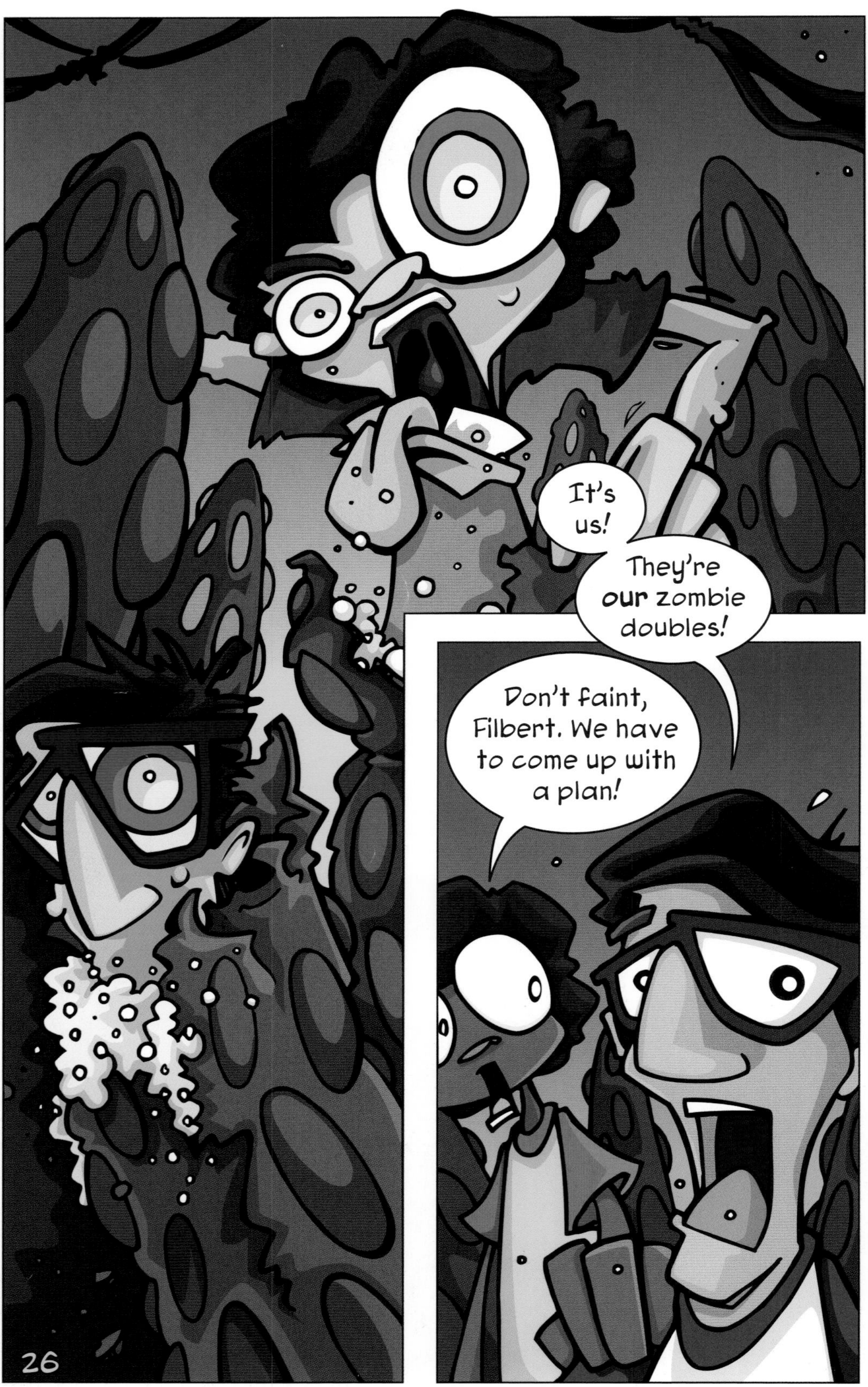
It's us!
They're **our** zombie doubles!
Don't faint, Filbert. We have to come up with a plan!

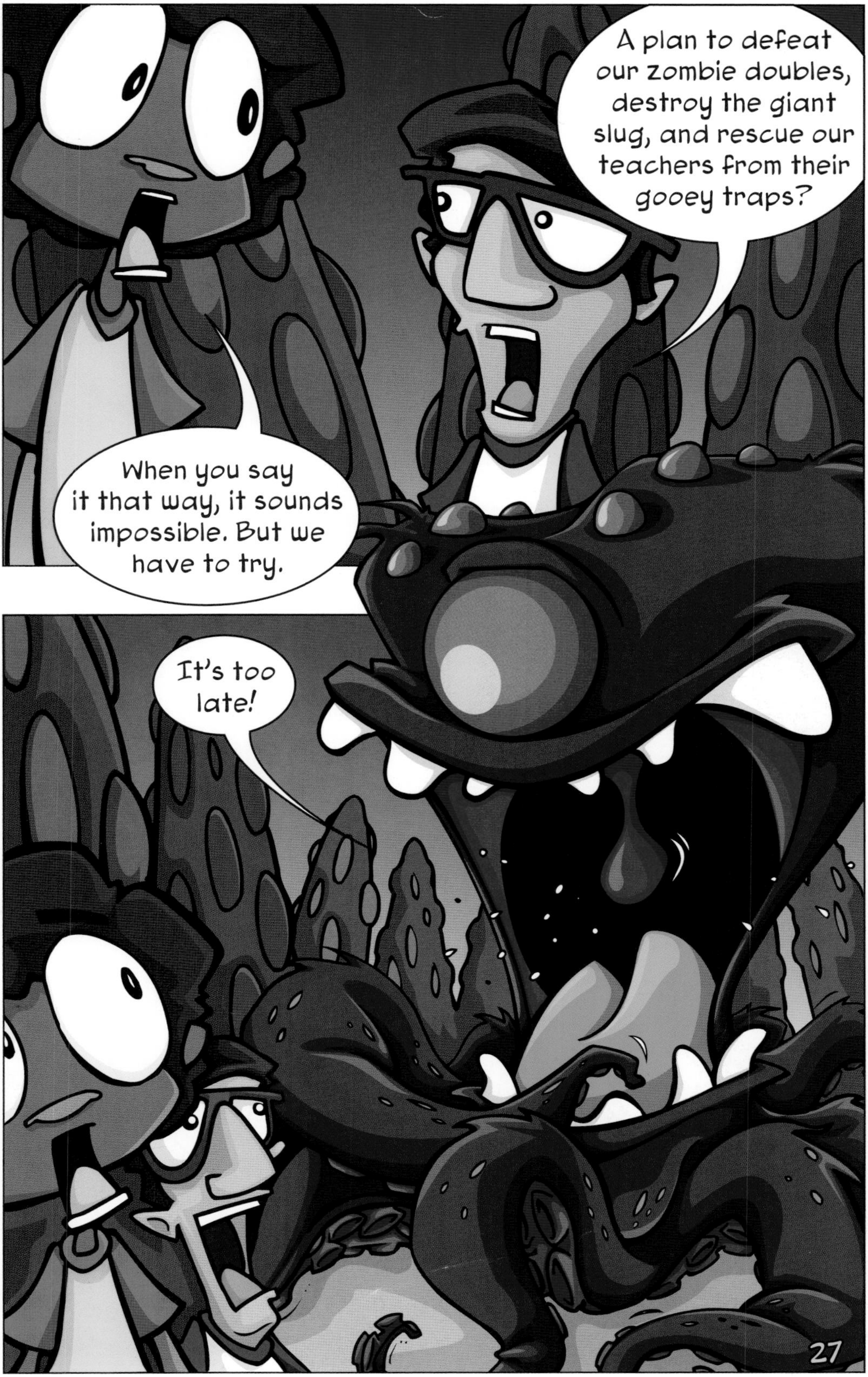
A plan to defeat our zombie doubles, destroy the giant slug, and rescue our teachers from their gooey traps?
When you say it that way, it sounds impossible. But we have to try.
It's too late!

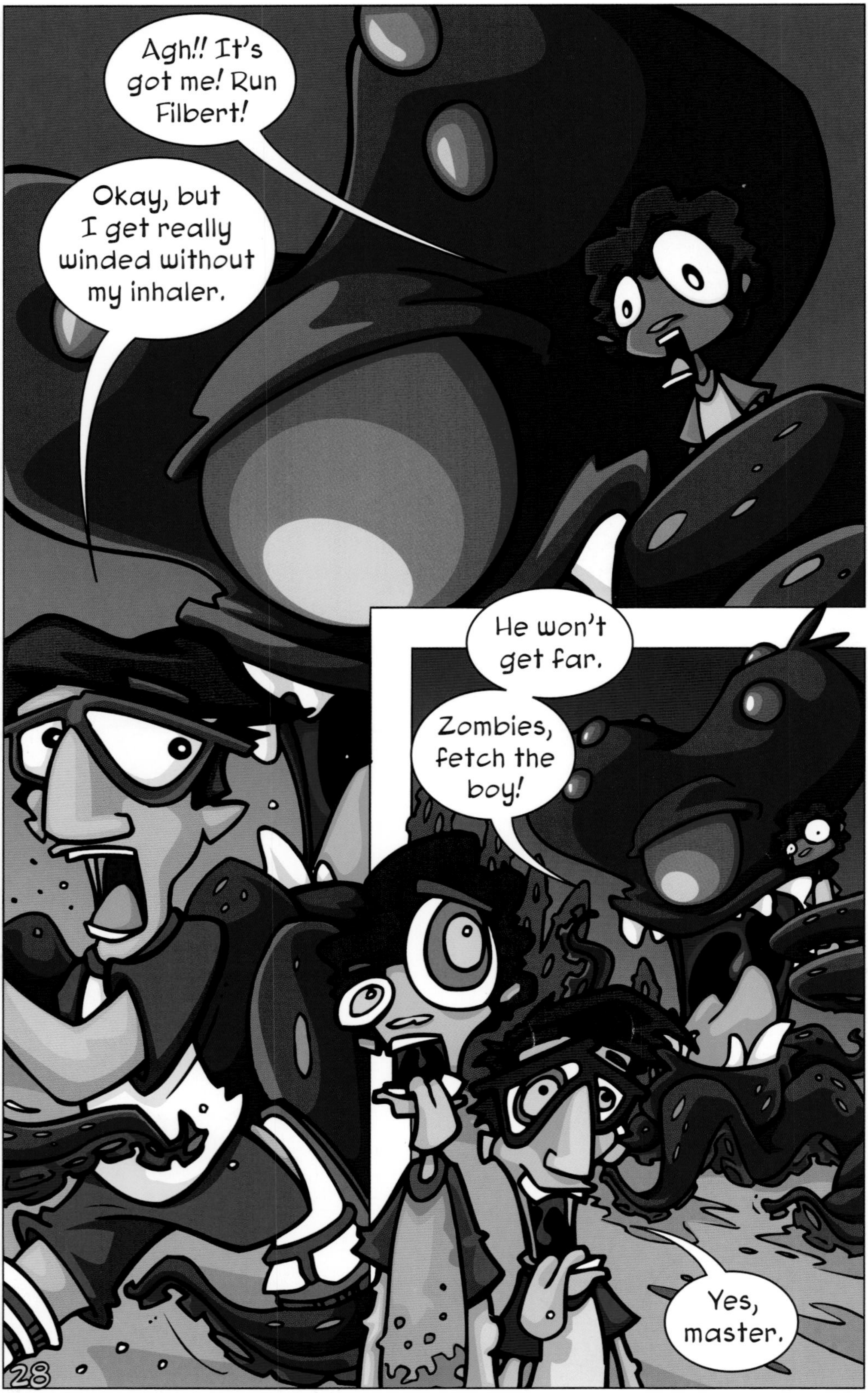
Agh!! It's got me! Run Filbert!
Okay, but I get really winded without my inhaler.
He won't get far.
Zombies, fetch the boy!
Yes, master.

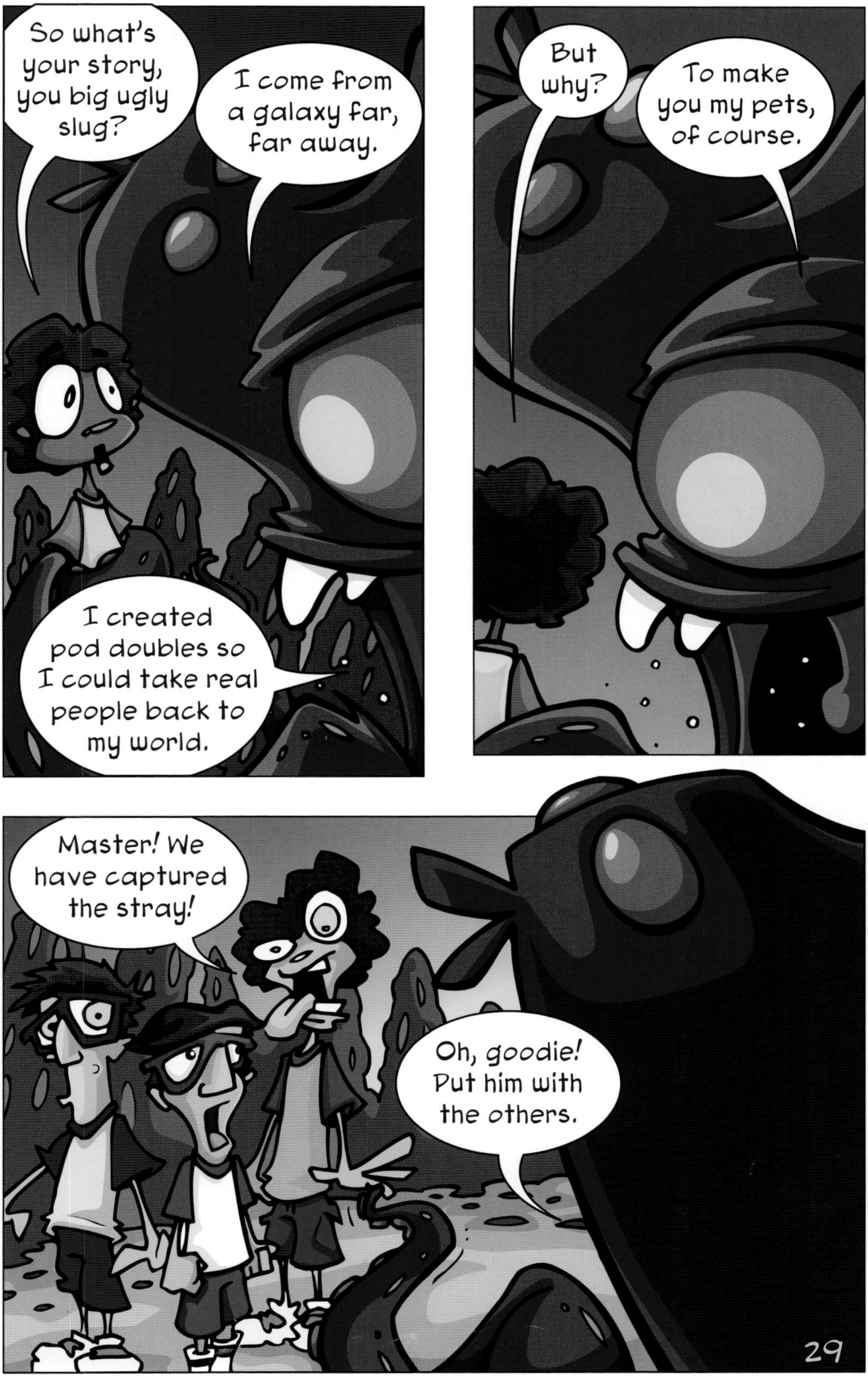
So what's your story, you big ugly slug?
I come from a galaxy far, far away.
I created pod doubles so I could take real people back to my world.
But why?
To make you my pets, of course.
Master! We have captured the stray!
Oh, goodie! Put him with the others.

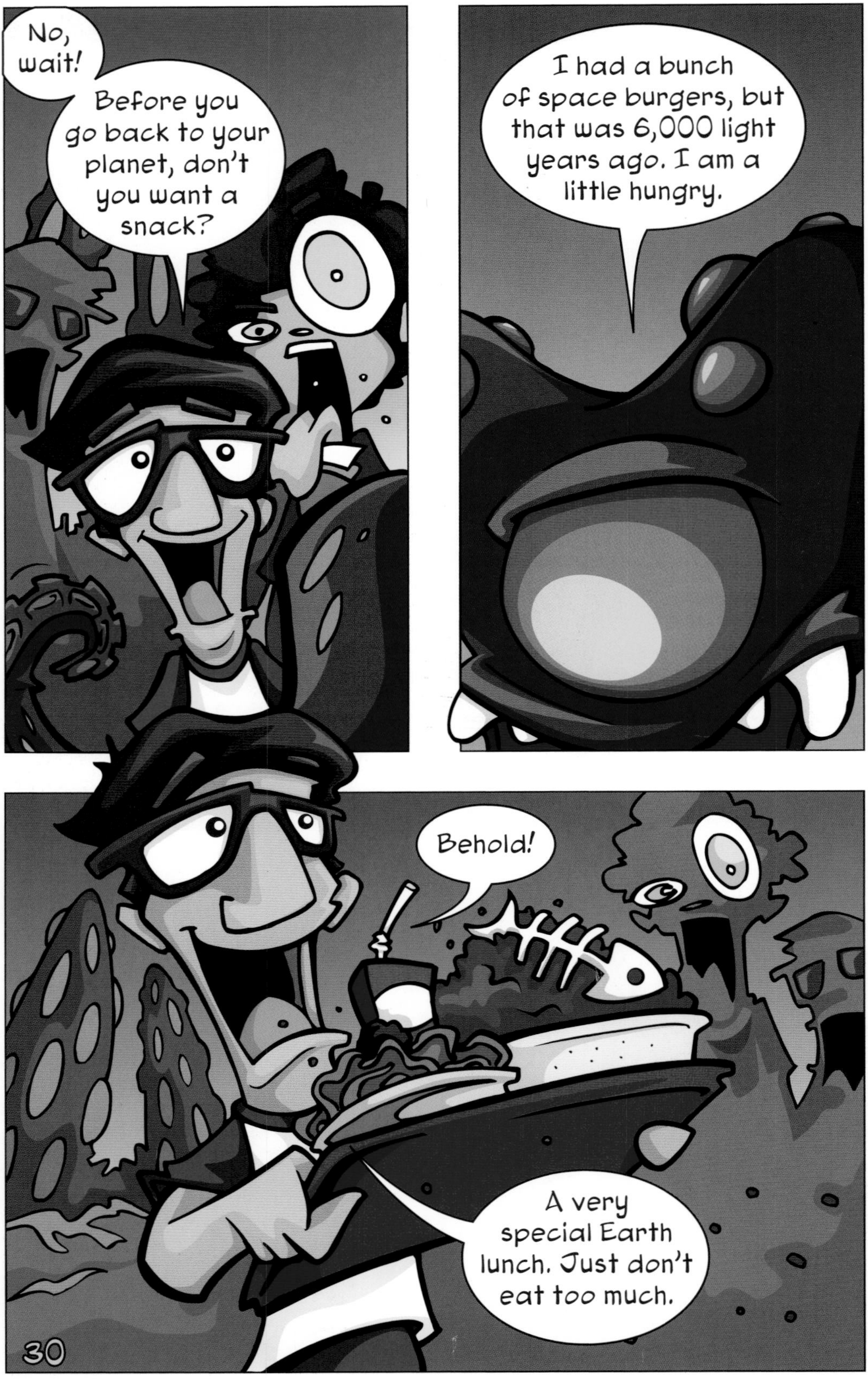
No, wait!
Before you go back to your planet, don't you want a snack?
I had a bunch of space burgers, but that was 6,000 light years ago. I am a little hungry.
Behold!
A very special Earth lunch. Just don't eat too much.

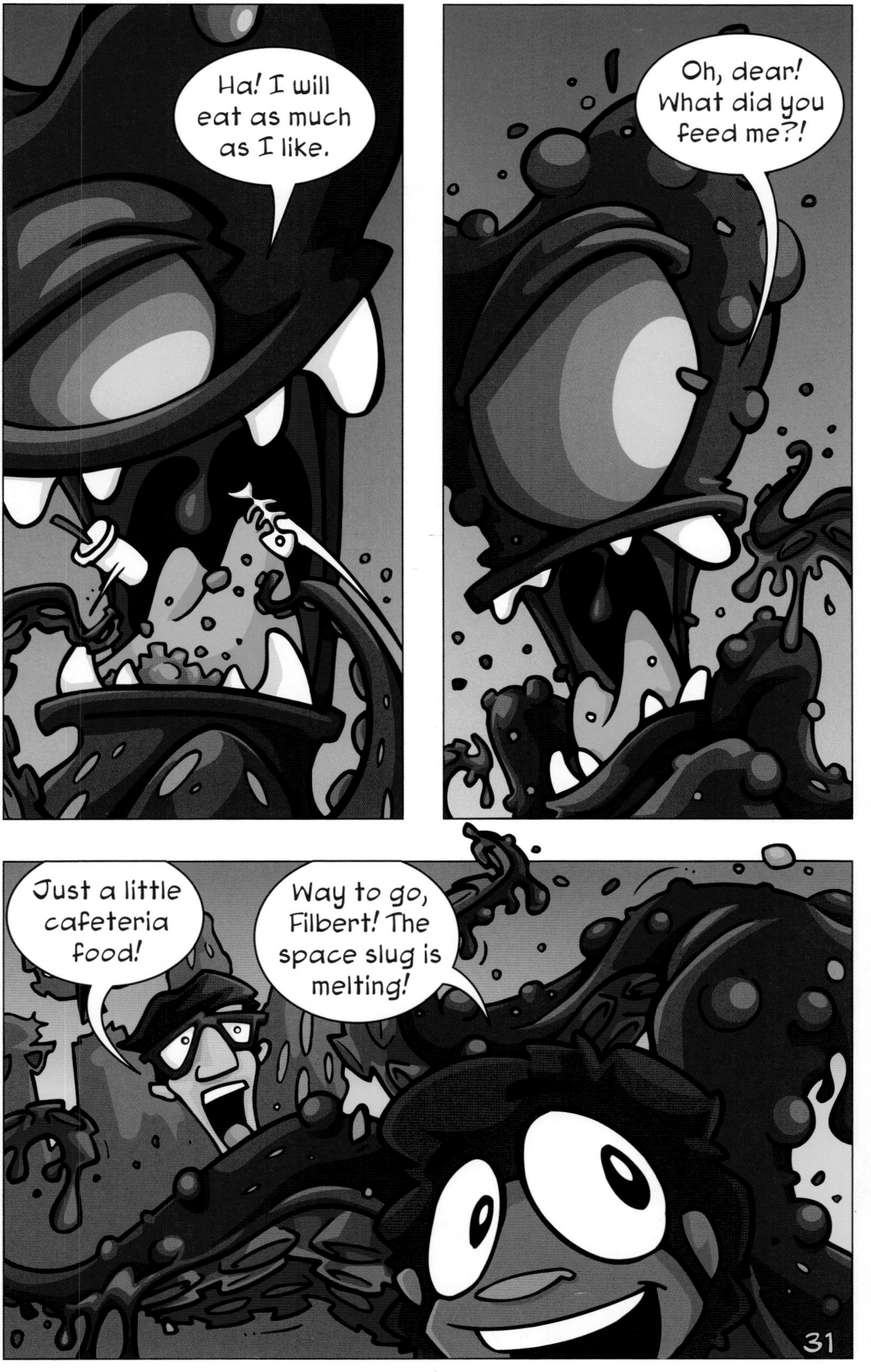

Ha! I will eat as much as I like.
Oh, dear! What did you feed me?!
Just a little cafeteria food!
Way to go, Filbert! The space slug is melting!

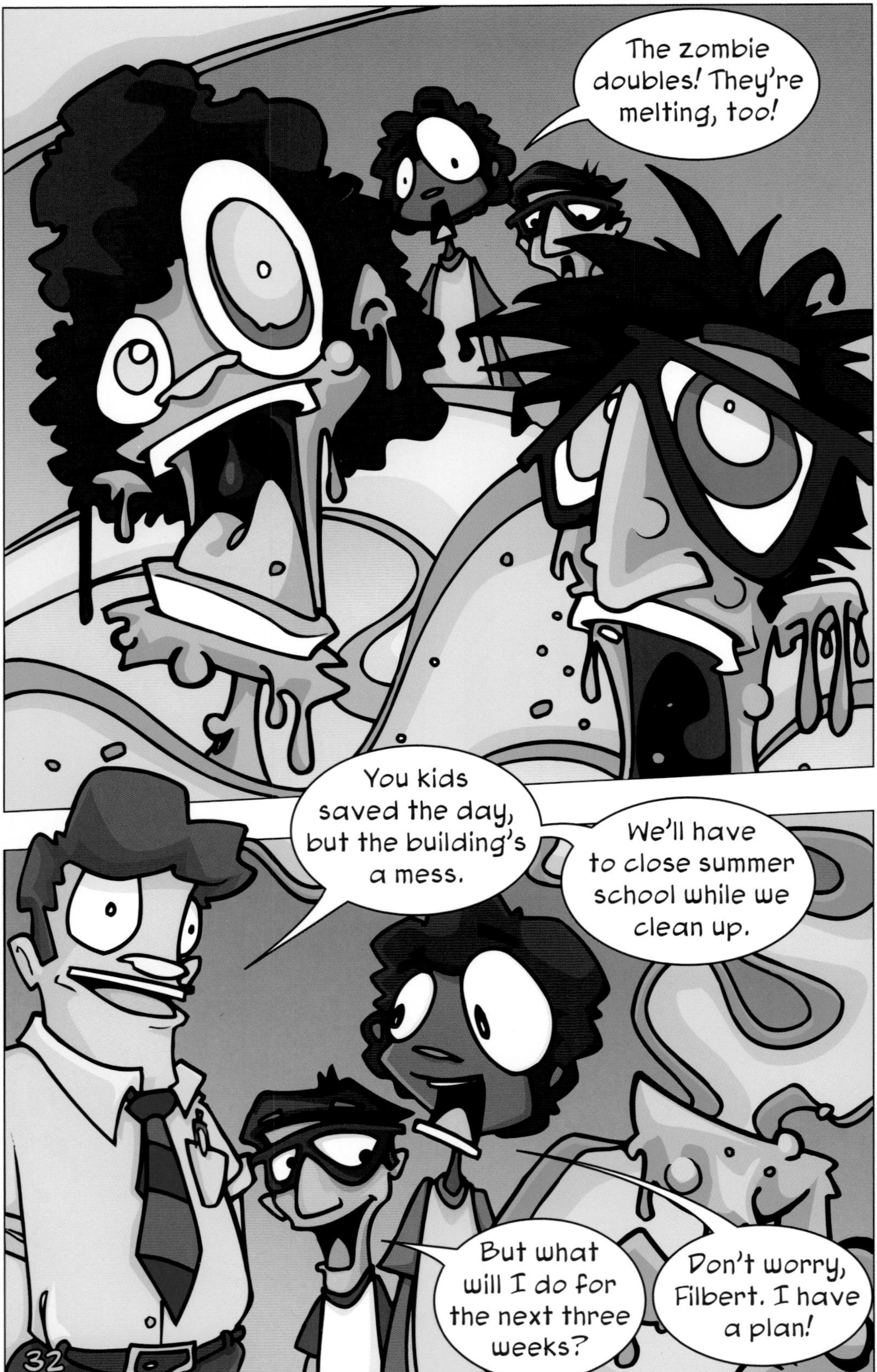
The zombie doubles! They're melting, too!
You kids saved the day, but the building's a mess.
We'll have to close summer school while we clean up.
But what will I do for the next three weeks?
Don't worry, Filbert. I have a plan!
32

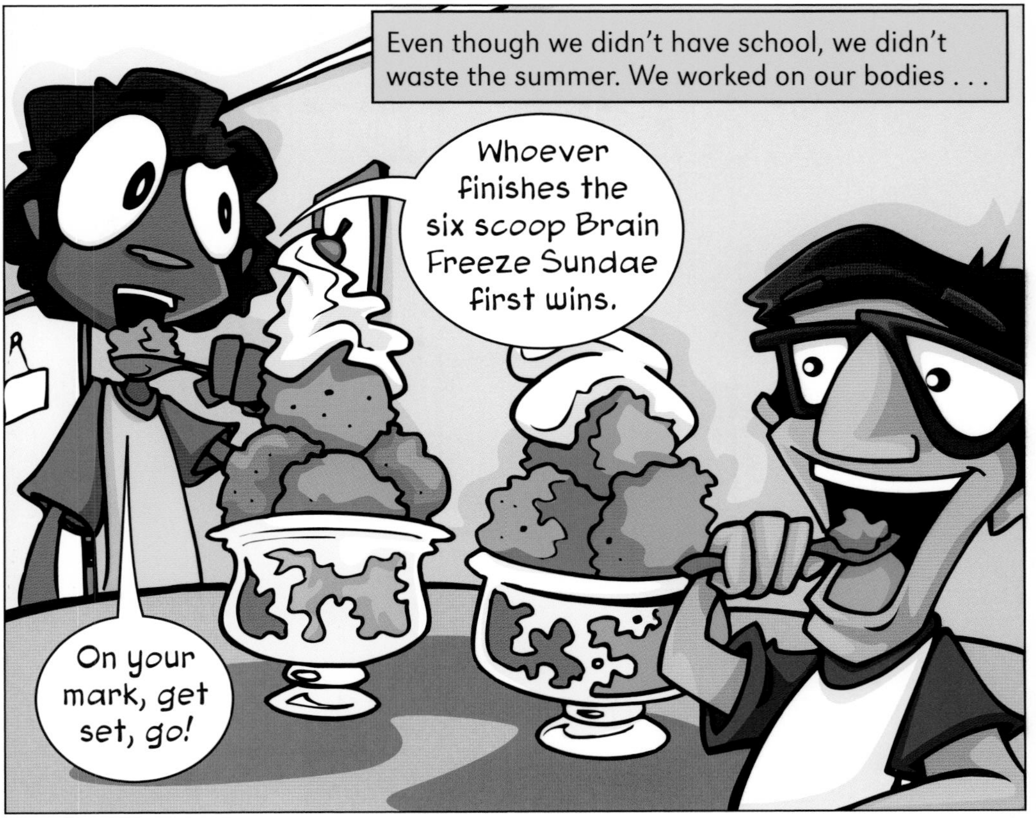
Even though we didn't have school, we didn't waste the summer. We worked on our bodies . . .
Whoever finishes the six scoop Brain Freeze Sundae first wins.
On your mark, get set, go!

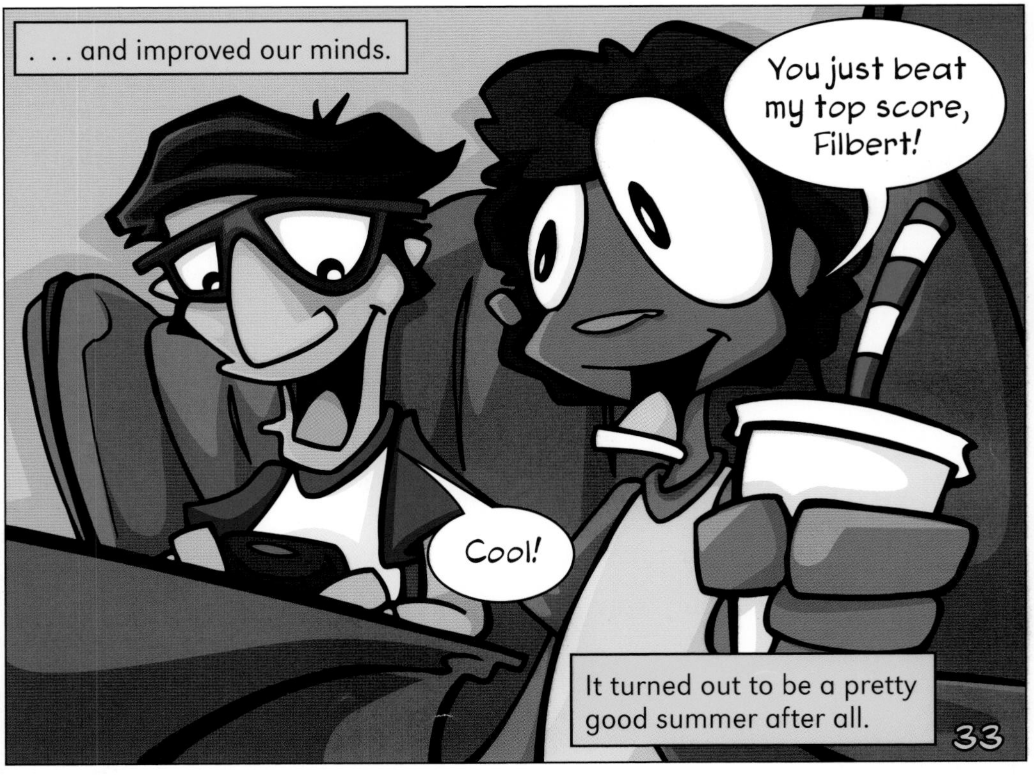
. . . and improved our minds.
You just beat my top score, Filbert!
Cool!
It turned out to be a pretty good summer after all.

ABOUT THE AUTHOR

Growing up, Scott Nickel wanted to be a comic book writer or a mad scientist. As an adult, he gets to do both. In his secret literary lab, Scott has created more than a dozen graphic novels for Stone Arch Books featuring time travelers, zombies, robots, giant insects, and mutant lunch ladies. Scott's *Night of the Homework Zombies* received the 2007 Golden Duck award for Best Science Fiction Picture Book. When not creating crazy comics, Scott squeezes in a full-time job as a writer and editor at Jim Davis's Garfield studio. He lives in Muncie, Indiana, with his wife, two teenage sons, and an ever-growing number of cats.

ABOUT THE ILLUSTRATOR

Matt Luxich started drawing at three years old. Although his parents didn't enjoy cleaning their son's cartoons off of the walls, they supported his talent. Years later, Luxich attended the Kubert School of Illustration and Animation in Dover, New Jersey. Today, he uses the skills he learned at school in his job as a freelance illustrator and designer, working for clients such as Golden Books and the Salvation Army. When he's not drawing, Luxich likes to eat cheese slices, play with toy robots, and walk his English Bulldog, Dover.

GLOSSARY

cafeteria (kaf-uh-TIHR-ee-uh)—a place where food is served at a counter and then taken to a table; a cafeteria is often called a lunchroom.

defeat (di-FEET)—to beat someone at a competition

encyclopedias (en-sye-kluh-PEE-dee-uhz)—those thick, dusty books in the library, which contain information on many different subjects

geography (jee-OG-ruh-fee)—the study of Earth, including its people, climate, and physical features

inhaler (in-HAY-lur)—a small device used to breathe in medicine through the mouth

permission (pur-MISH-uhn)—allowing someone to do something they ask to do

pioneer (pye-uh-NEER)—a person who explores new and unknown lands; the first settlers of the American West were pioneers.

zombie (ZOM-bee)—someone whose brain is controlled by another person; when you tell your friend to eat worms, and he does it, he is acting like a zombie.

MORE ABOUT ALIENS AND UFOs

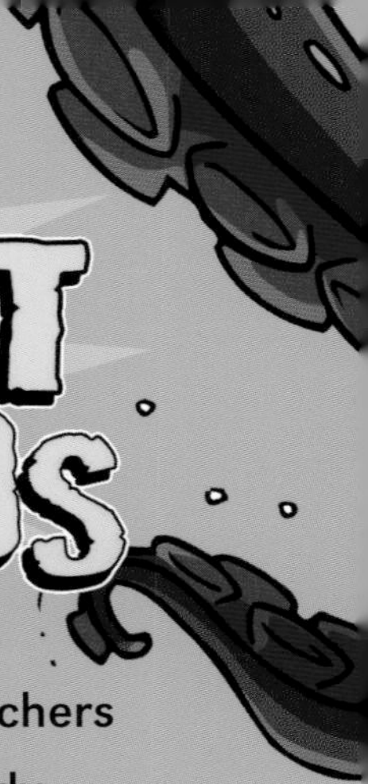

Could aliens really come to Earth and turn your teachers into homework-crazed creatures? Maybe they already have! Well, maybe not. But many people believe aliens have visited Earth thousands of times.

Every year, people around the world report seeing unidentified flying objects, also known as UFOs. Although most people see UFOs in the sky at night, their sizes and shapes often vary. Some report flying saucers or large objects shaped like triangles. Others have seen flashing lights, which are too bright to be airplanes.

Some believe UFO sightings have only happened recently. But in fact, people have believed in alien visitors for thousands of years. Ancient Mayans lived in Central America nearly 3,500 years ago. These people believed their gods came from the stars.

Many ancient artifacts and monuments are linked to aliens. The Great Pyramids in Egypt and Stonehenge in Britain are two of the most famous. Some believe humans could not have lifted the gigantic stones used to build these monuments. Instead, they claim creatures from another planet constructed the sites.

Perhaps the most famous alien sighting happened in Roswell, New Mexico, on June 14, 1947. That night, people reported seeing several "flying discs" in the sky. At a local ranch, farmer William "Mac" Brazel discovered the wreckage of a strange aircraft. The U.S. Army quickly cleaned up the debris, saying it was nothing more than a simple weather balloon. Many believe the Army found an alien spaceship and has tried to cover it up ever since.

After the sighting in Roswell, New Mexico, President Harry S. Truman created a top-secret group to investigate aliens and UFOs. This group is often known as the Majestic 12. Of course, since the group was top secret, the U.S. government denies that it ever existed.

So, have UFOs visited Earth? From 1947 to 1970, the U.S. Air Force investigated 12,618 UFO sightings in a program called Project Blue Book. When they had finished, the officials concluded that many of the sightings were hoaxes or simply stars in the sky. But even their scientists could not explain 701 of the reports. The question remains a mystery.

DISCUSSION QUESTIONS

1. How did Trevor's relationship with Filbert change throughout the book? Do you think Trevor liked Filbert at the beginning of the story? Do you think Trevor liked Filbert at the end of the story? Explain your answers using examples from the book.

2. On page 15, Trevor lied to get permission to leave the classroom. If he hadn't lied, the aliens might have taken over the school. Do you think he should still be punished for lying to his teacher? Explain.

3. This book was written and illustrated by two different people. If you had a choice, would you rather be an author or an illustrator? Explain your decision.

WRITING PROMPTS

1. Write your own alien adventure. What do your aliens look like? Are they good or evil? Describe how you would greet the aliens when they first arrive on Earth.

2. Pretend you are the author and write another tale about Trevor versus the zombies. Where will the zombies show up this time? The choice is up to you.

3. In this story, we learn that Trevor's friend, Filbert, loves school and encyclopedias. But we don't learn much else about him. Write your own story about Filbert's family, friends, pets, and hobbies.

INTERNET SITES

The book may be over, but the adventure is just beginning.

Do you want to read more about the subjects or ideas in this book? Want to play cool games or watch videos about the authors who write these books? Then go to FactHound. At *www.facthound.com*, you'll be able to do all that, and more. The FactHound website can also send you to other safe Internet sites.

Check it out!

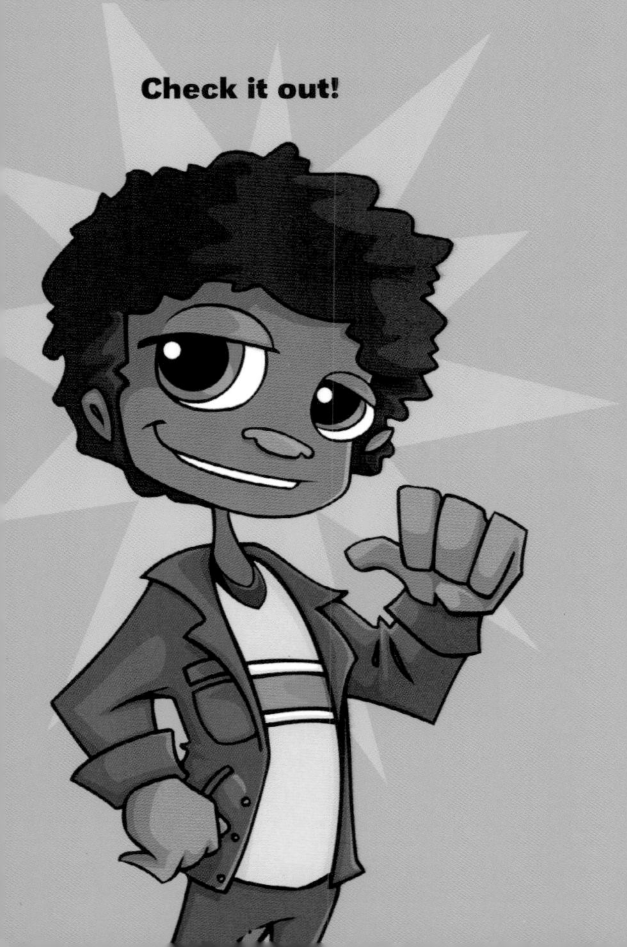